CUSTOMER CARE SKELETON PRESENTS

WE LIVING FAILURES

J. R. Santos

J.R. SANTOS

IF YOU LIKE IT, LEAVE A REVIEW !

CONTENTS

INTRODUCTION

Childhood only comes around once, and all that goes wrong stays with us.

No lack of writing material there! I see myself as a surrealist, trauma is the core of my strange stories.

Time is a Temple was my tackling of time as one such source of unappealing experiences. This collection explores another source: the impact people have on each other, especially when we're in our youth. How that weight is carried on, by us, the people around us and so on.

One of the seeds for this story collection was likely planted by a story in the *Time is a Temple* collection, a story called "They, Who Are the Future" but which, due to being too long, I have decided not to include in this collection. I started writing these stories back in 2020-2021, with the exceptions of "Toadie" and "Last Call to Casas" which date to 2023.

I wanted smaller stories, and to make this a fun ride, less stories also. I was told the previous collection proved a bit intimidating for new readers.

Enjoy!

"Children are like wet cement: whatever falls on them makes an impression."

– Haim Ginott (1922-1973), Psychologist

The Toy Trader

Times change but toys are toys. Wood, metal or plastic; traditional or modern, simple or complex, toys are toys and children like to play. With their wonderful imagination, anything can be a toy.

Carlos was eight years old and his brand new toy appeared to be a rock. He held it in his small hands with tremendous delight. It was perfectly shaped like a cube, as if crafted to be that way, to fit in a perfect square shaped hole. Carlos showed it to his friends and they agreed that it was a good rock.

They all played together and had a great time, with the other toys lined up at the end of their great adventures, plastic figures prostrated in worship of the rock as if it was an altar raised to honor a nameless and shapeless God. All the kids got a turn drawing on the rock using pens with felt tips, painting it in garish colors. It all became quite a mess, and the hours just slipped through the children's grasp.

By the time Carlos realized he had misplaced the rock, it was too late. He was quite upset with the thing's absence, certain that one of the others had taken it and so he cried to his parents of this injustice but nothing was done to amend it.

That night in his room with all his toys lined up, all his games and books, all these things felt like they were not enough, not enough at

all. After all, none of them were that stone cube. Carlos cried and he
pouted, and tossed around all the board games, teddy bears, action
figures and racing cars.

What a mess he had made of his room.

"What a mess you made," a voice said. Carlos looked around
feeling very scared. **"Why, your parents should punish you. Yes,
you've been very naughty."**

Carlos looked and the door to his room was open a little bit; just
enough for someone to peek in from the dark hallway outside. All he
saw from beyond the door was the shadows, and a single eye staring
without blinking.

**"Is that any way to treat your toys? Why, I wish I had toys like
yours. They all look so fun. All I have is this boring rock."**

Carlos' eyes opened wide, as he stumped back against his bed. "My
rock?" he wondered out loud.

"No." said the voice. **"M Y! R O C K!"** It said slow and loud,
enunciating each word very clearly. **"I found it and wrote my name
on it. See?"**

The door opened a little more and a rock, just like the one Carlos
had lost, emerged slowly from the shadows. One of the sides was a
symbol that Carlos couldn't read, though he had learned a lot of letters
and could already read many words.

"It looks like my rock." Carlos pouted feebly.

"Well. It isn't." Said the voice. **"But I could trade you. If you
want the rock this bad, you just let me have all your toys and
games."**

Carlos did not like that offer one bit.

"Greedy, aren't we?" the voice asked, his single eye never moving.
"I'll take my rock then. Goodnight."

The rock went back into the shadows. The eye in the dark blinked once and was gone. Carlos went to bed, too scared to go out and find the voice and the stolen toy. Next day he tried to tell his parents about the voice, but they ignored him. At school, he told no one, afraid of being ignored or made fun of. The other children had toys and games of their own and were happy to play with him and make up all sorts of adventures. Someone mentioned the rock, and Carlos was sad again. The kids found new rocks to play with but none were good. None were shaped like a cube.

Carlos started a fight that day. Oliver, his best friend, didn't understand why Carlos was unhappy with the absence of his new toy when it was just a dumb rock. Many angry words were shouted and the boys wrestled and ended up hurt, which thrilled everyone else to no end since fights were such fun things to watch.

The day ended with bruises, a sore ego and a great deal of admonishment from the parents who were very disappointed and had expected better from their boys.

That night found him in an even sourer mood. All his toys had been taken and locked up in the basement. A cruel punishment and unfair to boot, at least in his eyes.

"Psst." Carlos looked from his bed, jumping in place. From the slightly open door, the eye peeked out again, just like the night before. **"Why are your toys in my room?"**

Carlos didn't understand, and he answered, uncertainly. "They're in the basement."

"I know," the voice said. **"I woke up and they were all there. Did you change your mind? I don't mind giving you the rock like I promised."**

Carlos closed his hands into fists, a thing he did whenever he wanted to focus but was too nervous to do so properly. The toys were in the basement and his parents would get them back, like they always did.

The time was right, ripe for trickery.

"Yes," lied Carlos, "they're all for you if you give me back my rock."

The voice sounded a little offended. **"It's my rock! M I N E!"**

The rock appeared, as colorful and perfectly cubical as before. It was dragged gently forward from the shadows by a long, thin and twisted hand, into the room illuminated by the moon's pale glare creeping through the window pane. A matching wrist was attached to the hand that dragged it, rather than pushing it. Twisted, with more knuckles than any human fingers ought to need.

"But I'll trade you if you're sure. It's only fair."

All his toys for the painted rock was not fair at all, and Carlos knew it well. He wasn't scared of the voice as much as the night before, not if this was someone he could trick so easily. He nodded cheerfully and raced from his bed, his bare feet making no noise when touching the carpet. He greedily held the rock in both his hands.

He looked back and the eye was gone. He waited and no sounds came from the corridor outside his room.

Carlos went back to his bed, excited with the thrill of outsmarting the voice his parents didn't believe in. He held his precious toy close to him and fell asleep.

The next he went to school with the rock hidden in his backpack, ready to show Oliver how wrong he was, and excited to play with everyone again.

But no one played with him. The other kids looked at him weird and no one wanted to touch or even look at the rock. Carlos stared disappointed at his treasure. It *did* look different from what he remembered. It was still a perfect cube but all red now, with a weird looking letter drawn on one side.

He played with it, but got bored quickly. It was just a rock after all. The voice may have been right; this had been the voice's own toy and not the one Carlos had lost. He fumbled with the thing in his hands, turning it around, but the rock did not change, and it was starting to smell weird.

The playground of the school was big and had some grass and trees, so he found a hole on the ground by one of the big trees and threw the rock into it, right under one of the big roots. He apologized to Oliver right after and everything seemed better. His life was returning to normal.

But his toys were gone. All of them. Mom and dad kept them locked up, leaving Carlos no other recourse but to weep in boredom.

Hours stretched into what felt like days. He wanted his toys and games back, and felt almost brave enough to try to pry the basement door open. He snuck to it at the dead of night but started to change his mind as he got closer.

Later, standing a bit away, staring at the well-shut door, he heard muffled noises from beyond this great barrier, from the depths of the basement. The boy inched a little closer, and tried peeking under the door, in that tiny bit of space between it and the floor. As soon as he did, his eyes adjusting to that sliver of inky blackness, he saw that single eye looking back.

"**What do you want?**" The voice inquired rudely. "**I'm playing with my toys, leave me alone.**"

Carlos felt immensely upset at being denied what was his. "I want them back," he protested.

"**They're mine and I like them. You can go play with the one I traded you,**" the voice replied, now sounding more bored than angry.

"I don't want it. I want my toys back." Carlos was starting to feel dizzy from the exhausting interaction with the thing that took his toys. He got back up and stared at the doorknob as if waiting for it to turn and allow him in.

"So what? They're mine now. If you want to give me my toy back, I'll take it but I won't give yours back." After a long pause the voice added **"Maybe if you trade something better... I'll let you have them back. Or some of them, at least."**

Carlos held back a distressed sob that had started to build up in anxious anger.

"What do *you* want?" He asked in frustrated despair to the voice.

"A puppy."

Carlos held his head with both his hands, tugging at his own hair. "But I don't have a puppy!"

"Too bad. I only trade for stuff I haven't played with yet. I can play games with a puppy, even dress it up, and read to it all my favorite stories. Go away and don't come back unless you have one."

Carlos stood, still in front of the door but the voice would not speak again. He gave up after a while and left, afraid his parents would punish him even more, somehow, if they found him out of his room at night.

***

Next day, working up some courage, Carlos asked for his toys back. His parents said no. He asked for a puppy and his dad laughed and then said no. Before leaving for school, he asked his mother if there was someone living in the basement, which made her look at him in a weird way, but then she said no and shooed him out of the house. He wondered what he could possibly do. As the week went on, coming back home turned into the worst thing ever. Every night he would sneak to the basement door, only to receive no answer.

Unaware of what had happened, his parents assumed that taking his toys had made Carlos enjoy his time in school all the more and congratulated themselves on a job well done. They saw no reason to change something that was working out so well, and decided Carlos might never see his toys again.

No puppies though. A goldfish was suggested as an alternative, and Carlos whispered this to the voice through a shut basement door.

"Fish are boring." This was all the voice cared to reply, and nothing else was said. Carlos knew this was true, which was why he could say nothing in turn.

Oliver and the other classmates had become very close friends with Carlos however; an upside to Carlos doing his best to escape the long boring hours and dark weird nights. He had become more receptive to his schoolmates and their games rather than forcing his usual ones upon them.

A sleepover was arranged as a reward for Carlos' good behavior. Oliver would come over and bring his own games.. As soon as Oliver was sleeping deeply, however, Carlos snuck out to the basement door and told the voice what he could offer.

"I don't have a puppy. But my friend bought his games. You could play with them and give me back mine."

The voice didn't answer.

"It's been so long! Aren't you bored? You're playing with them all alone in there."

The voice sighed.

"It's true, I am all alone down here. I don't have a friend like you do."

A bright idea filled Carlos' head, and his lungs felt full of fresh air; a hope so real and so close he could almost touch it.

"You can have my friend if you let me have my games and toys back!" He almost shouted and perhaps did, forgetting how late it was and immediately shushed himself, holding his breath for a long moment, expecting his parents to show up and tell him to go back to bed.

They didn't. After a long pause the voice wondered aloud **"I wouldn't have any games to play with my friend, if I gave yours back."**

Carlos clapped his hands excitedly, but not too hard to avoid making too much noise.

"He has his own games! He'll bring them along!"

The voice was silent which made Carlos very nervous, but eventually the voice said yes. The deal was made, and Carlos would have his toys back if he could get his soon to be former friend down to the basement.

Waking Oliver up was the hardest part. Carlos almost thought his friend was pretending to sleep, and so shook him harder, a bit too roughly. Soon they were both up and he helped his friend grab his games, so that they then tip-toed all the way to the basement door, which the boys found wide open.

It was too dark to see. Carlos rushed in, looked back and urged his friend along. As they both entered the darkness, all light and sound went away. Carlos opened his eyes. He had never stopped walking down the basement stairs but still, blinking blindly between downward steps, he found himself back at the basement door, his back to it.

Alone, he turned around to see it close slowly, ever so slowly, until the door was shut with a click. Carlos was left confused, looking down at his arms which had been carrying all those fun things, but now carried nothing. He felt sleepy and everything became blurry as if part of a strange dream. He walked back to his room and found Oliver wasn't there anymore, but all of the toys and games the voice had taken were back. Even the red cube made of rock, sitting on a shelf close to the window. He went back to his bed, and was soon asleep.

His parents weren't happy. Oliver's parents weren't happy either. No one could find him and the police eventually showed up.

Dad was so angry that Carlos thought his toys would be taken from him again but no one remembered to take them this time, or even that they had even been taken before.

"He was in your room! Where did he go? His toys, his clothes! Where did he go?"

Carlos simply replied "The basement," and so everyone searched the basement again and again but Oliver wasn't there, nor were his toys or clothes. A nice lady, who told Carlos she was a cop but had no uniform, noticed the red rock and asked if it was his. Carlos lied without hesitation and said that it wasn't, so the lady put the rock in a transparent bag and took it. Then again, perhaps it was no lie but for one of omission. Had the voice not claimed it was the owner of the rock, and not Carlos? It was better this way.

Everyone was sad and tired, and after the police left, the fights started. Carlos' parents argued with each other all the time, shouting and being scary at first, and then just being very boring. With all of this, Carlos didn't even think about the basement again, or the voice. Months went by, Carlos turned nine years old, and one day his mother told him his father was gone.

"To the basement?" he wondered aloud. He couldn't remember the last time he had thought of it, or cared about what his choices had caused. His mom gave him that funny look he didn't like, then explained to him what a divorce was.

By the end of the next month, they had left the house.

JENNY GREEN

It was foggy most times of the year and when it wasn't foggy it was damp. Everything was green and pretty, when you could actually see it, and the notion drew enough tourists during summer, only for them to be met with rain.

"Can't you do anything?" the bolder tourists would ask. The locals couldn't or they would have. The humidity ate through everything, rotting and molding away people's health, their food, and even their homes. Life here was a constant fight against nature, and nature always won.

Dani spent most of their time bored. The internet connection was bad all year round and Dani's friends were out of town half the time on some holiday or other - the rest moved out with their families and never came back. It would be a ghost town sooner or later, just a handful of buildings populated by tourists and a skeleton crew to entertain them.

Dani wouldn't mind leaving too but they couldn't, unless their mom could find a job to pay for it. Almost sixteen, Dani would offer to help and try to work at least a part time, to kill some time if nothing else. But the jobs were few and most of them were just pandering to the uncaring crowds. Aimlessly wandering down one of the old roads leading from the town to the verdant surrounding swamplands, someone greeted them.

"Dani! Over here!" An old man waved and smiled.

"Hi grandpa!" They hugged, both happy for the comfort of a familiar face in their ever-emptying town. "What are you up to today?"

The old man laughed. "I should be the one asking that, you rascal! What happened to going to school?"

Dani made a face. "They let us out early because a wall crumbled up."

Dani's grandfather cringed. "Everyone all right? How did that even happen?"

"Yeah, everyone's ok, but they might not let us back in the school for days. Everyone says it's the mold inside the walls."

Dani's grandfather mouthed silently the word 'mold' and looked into the distance, out toward the bogs.

"One of these days..." The old man looked back down, focused but tired. "Just the mold and this insufferable weather. But if it was Jenny..."

"Jenny Green?" A local legend that no one but the old folks believed in, a ghost of the bog. "I think the school was just old. Jenny can come over and build us a new school though."

The old man looked sad now, and a little disappointed. "You don't have to believe it, but Jenny was real. She would have been my age now. Have I ever told you that?"

Dani nodded.

"Well, she would! She's not alive but she's not dead either. No one found her body, but she's in there. Maybe under a tree, or sunk into the peat and grime."

He started walking back to town and Dani followed.

"When I was your age, I tried to find her body with some friends. It had been two years and we had all seen her ghost, glowing green and stinking of rot, growing mold everywhere she touched." Dani's grandfather let out a long, and deeply tired sigh. "We used to believe that the body needed to be cremated and a prayer said over the ashes in order to send off the spirit. We almost died in the marshes trying to help her move on.

"There was swamp gas, poisonous animals and just the weather itself. It's always wet. Always. We all walked out soaked, a couple of us even caught fevers after that trip."

A morbid idea crossed Dani's mind.

"What if she's in the school? Her body, I mean?"

"No, Dani. Jenny's body is in the bogs where she died. But her spirit is everywhere. It's why some kids were born with dark green marks on them. You remember Eva? From the bakery? She was the talk of town, the first one to get those big marks all over her back. Everyone was worried, but she was lucky to grow up fine in spite of it.."

Dani thought about it and couldn't help but comment. "She breathes funny."

"Yes, well, she is still alive. That's healthy enough. You're right, of course. She has some problems, but so does everyone else. This place has all the problems and no solutions." They stopped on the street with plenty of noise, the few local children wandering about, as well as a few tourist families. "Folk who come and go, have their fun if any and see no ghosts. Be like them, Dani. Never go there at night, not to prove me wrong, and never to prove me right. Had we found Jenny..."

They hugged again, the old man drifting into his own memories and growing silent for a long moment. "Go home. It will be dark soon."

***

The old man prayed, turning over the rosary in his hands, again and again, as the curtains of time were pulled back; the weight of his guilt tethered to the ends. It was heavy with the burden from his childhood mistakes. He had been so young. Jenny and him, they had both become lost in the verdant labyrinth but Jenny had been the one who tripped and broke her neck.

He had been known to be reckless, sometimes even awful, and he knew then, no one would believe him - that she had made a mistake. That it wasn't his fault. He simply wandered until he found his way back home and when he did, he never said a word. Jenny's parents weren't particularly liked, but when they sounded the alarm, their child lost, everyone helped in the searches. Her body was never found. A vagrant was blamed for her disappearance, and it was said a mob had disposed of him.

He had two bodies on his conscience from that day onward, but only Jenny's ghost followed him out of the green.

A vengeful ghost of a spiteful child, who had made herself visible to him, a green glow in the mist and calling through the dark of the night. Her neck had not mended in death, her head lolled sideways and mushrooms grew from her eye sockets and mouth, as well as from moldy patches of her ragged clothes and bloated bluish skin.

She felt her way across town, and all she touched soon grew mold and became broken, ruined by her infectious curse. Decades had stretched long beyond reason, people were born and others died, but all had been touched by this evil growing its roots deeper into every-thing and everyone. Dani had been half right - Jenny had been to the school, perhaps even long enough to be found. Not buried there, but still present, hopefully in a body that the old man could destroy.

He found trails all over and the signs grew harder to ignore the closer he got to the old building they had both known half a century ago. He sat aside and prayed no matter if God chose to forgive him or not. For too long had he allowed this evil, but was prepared to fight it at last.

Dani's grandfather wore around his neck the rosary that had been his mother's. He picked up the gas mask and the flame thrower, the weapon's tank strapped around him like a backpack, heavy with the promise of a painful death.

These were souvenirs of a war that had never happened, a time when black market military goods circulated and everyone spent what little they could afford on self defense. They had expected soldiers to march down their streets and knock down their doors. There had been raids, ever so long ago, in the neighboring villages, but it seemed as this place had its own evils to deal with. The old man left his home at the dead of night, as the mists had started to swirl about, remembering the better days. Him and Jenny had been thick as thieves, stealing eggs from neighbors, exploring the nearby wilderness and finding new ways to worry everyone with new antics.

Maybe they had been too close, lost themselves too fast in each other's company, becoming too wild for their own good. Jenny's father would have beaten him to death had he got the chance, but he had disappeared in the days after. Likely, he had gone to search for his little girl again, only to be lost to the deadly swamps. He had been a harsh man, but in the end, he had tried his best. His wife did not seem worried by his disappearance, but continued to grief her lost daughter for the rest of her days.

His mind forced back to the present, the old man walked the empty streets as the fog swelled. Some such nights were guaranteed to find everyone indoors, even the tourists. Even these careless visitors were wary of becoming lost, or of breathing something hazardous. Government specialists had declared it safe, within reason, but people knew better than to follow advice from uncaring state officials and their vague statements.

Having lived there all his life, he knew where to go even in such blinding fog. With the world half hidden by the dense haze, it was too late to turn by the time he saw it. Just a few streets away from the school, stood a dark figure much too large to be Jenny. It moved slowly and as it approached, and the old man could see it looked swollen. He shrank in horror once he was close enough to see it well.

A grown man, bloated, rotting, and oozing, marched slowly in the direction of the school. Dozens of black mushrooms grew from the dark green layers of mold that seem to compose most of the creature's mass. The old man turned his flame thrower and blasted the deadly flame and heat onto the animated corpse, which did not react, but simply kept going until it had burned and melted so much it could not move anymore. As the corpse gave in, falling into a growing puddle made of its own burning sludge, it did not scream. No one came out of their homes to find the source of the fire, the smoke, or at least that of the terrible smell.

Jenny hadn't been the only one coming back. How many decades' worth of bodies had piled under the bogs? He had never realized it had gotten this bad, that there were so many others. Had he been too focused on his own guilt? Too obsessed with a world in which his sins were the center of everything? This thing had ignored him for decades but could have intentionally pursued others on those many, many nights.

Spread out, becoming infrequent enough they could be blamed on carelessness there were so many missing who could go unaccounted for as fuel for the green.

He found others as he neared the school. Dozens, too misshapen and far beyond recognition.. They must have been people he had known, as he had lived his whole life in the small town. But they were too far gone for him to be sure. He simply burned them and moved on, praying he had enough fuel to deal with everyone.

There always seemed to be more, but all ignored him as they continued spreading their rot where they went. The school, or what the old man could see of it, looked like it had aged a hundred years in one night, mold crawling like tendrils all the way up the walls, and eating at the ceiling.

Illuminated only by the eerie glow of the mist, he heard glass shattering and saw the brief reflection of the falling pieces, followed by chunks of the crumbling walls. All of it was falling away, being torn apart piece by piece as metal rusted, wood rotted, and the horde moved in. Jenny was nowhere in sight.

The corpses moved inside to the crumbling building. Too many, far too many for one old man. He stopped purging them with flames, his tank feeling too light. He needed to save whatever was left. A terrible instinct told him to move in, to look inside the school.

***

He ran in, and it felt like time was being made to turn back, forced to oppose its natural flow. He was young again, running down the halls and Jenny was there. It was always like they were two halves of the same person, able to feel each other close before they would even see each other. It was her, always. It had to be. The door to the classroom was gone – the one they had known so well in their young days. She was there, sitting at her place in the classroom some forty years later, a stagnant reflection of what had once been.

He stood in front of her, looking down. Time had transformed her, but enough was left that he was sure. He had to be.

Like a ghost limb, gone, yet he felt her presence.

"Jenny?" he called in a croaked muttering, again and again he called her name. What had once been Jenny simply sat in her seat, forearms resting on the table in front of her, as the black mold spread and everything fell apart around them.

He walked to the seat and table right next to Jenny's, what had been his place in his childhood. He sat down on a chair that was now too small for him. He looked at Jenny and reached out with a gloved hand. She never looked at him, but her arm moved and a small hand, mangled by time and weather found its way to him and rested on his palm.

He cried, sobbing uncontrollably as his body shook with grief and the unbearable weight of his guilt.

What was she? He would never know what had dragged itself out from Jenny's grave, a haunting echo or a corpse vessel to something beyond his understanding. He knew he had no time to think of it as he felt the damp spread through his glove, and he tried to blink away the tears that blinded him.

Letting go of her hand, he stood up again, but fell as his left leg sank into the crumbling floor. Panicked and unable to free himself, he aimed his flame thrower at Jenny. She had not moved, holding her hand out as if it was still resting on his. He cried and shouted, and the minutes felt like hours. He knew his time was up as the ceiling began

to fall around them, debris crashing down and hitting with the weight
h of boulders.

His thoughts went to Dani. What would happen if this curse didn't
end here with him? He was breathing faster now, panicked, as he
struggled to take the flamethrower's fuel tank from his back. The
classroom was crumbling down faster. He finally slipped it free and
right under Jenny. He said one last prayer, and closed his eyes and
pulled the trigger.

The anticipation was terrible, as was the heat of the flame as it
burned through wood, and heated the metal of the tank. He shouted
an apology. To Jenny, to his family, to everyone he had known and
lost.

The blast was sharp, deafening thunder. Burning hot metal shards
flew away cutting through flesh and bone. The fire followed in a
blinding wave and the searing went unfelt as it met only dead flesh,
uncaring mold, and the falling wreckage. The old man would never
know it but the bodies did stop moving then, like puppets whose
strings had been severed. The building crumbled in crushing them,
and soon the fire spread and cleansed away all remains. They were all
gone as the mist cleared and the flames raised higher and higher.

Morning would come as always, timid sunlight breaking through a
hazy horizon, to meet the ashes and burnt ruins. The firefighter crew
was joined by a handful of helpful locals who fought back the flames
once they had caught wind of it.

They contemplated but would only ever gain questions, for ashes
and blackened bones could not speak.

BUCK TOOTH

Come them haints
Come them devils
On wing and foot they come
From the forest
From the hill
We hide
And stand still
When they come
When they come

Farm life was great for those lucky enough to have others do all the hard work. It left these chosen few all the free time needed to find as many cows they could tip; steal all the eggs they could carry from every coop, and climb up any of the trees that came across their path. There was a school, but there wasn't much to learn, or at least not much expected of the kids in general.

Very few people from these farmlands went on to more academic endeavors, most expecting a little more from the local children then for them to learn counting and reading well enough to help with the work fated to keep them busy for all of their future adult lives. That work was the one constant, the toil that would fill every day of all of their lives until they eventually dropped dead of old age, exhaustion or a heart attack.

Back then the local school was just a little building; a tiny thing with enough room for a class, one grumpy teacher and the occasional punishment administered without hesitation. All the kids knew each other much like their parents knew each other as well, and their grandparents and so on.

Willy, Billy and Tilly were not the most creative nor creatively named of the class, but they didn't need to be. They spent most of their time together and they were always trouble.

The trio would walk home together and have their own little adventures, and though life was far from perfect, to them their world was happy and straight forward which made it as close to perfect as it would ever be. On their walks in the country, keeping to the side of the dirt road they knew so well, surprises were rare.

The best they could recall included the times when they had seen foxes crossing their path looking for the nearby woods, or the nearest chicken coops; and the other, when they had seen little ducks waddling towards where an old pond used to be; but this is the story of when they saw the thin haired child with dirt caked, grayish skin.

All three of them were scared at the sight of this child. They couldn't tell with certainty if the child was a boy or a girl, though by the way it dressed, Billy assumed it was a boy and the others followed suit. The gray boy looked at them with weird dark eyes and the one massive tooth, so big and deformed it protruded from the child's lower lip almost digging itself into the left cheek. He then turned his gaze back to his cupped hands as he sat again mirthlessly facing the road, his back against an old sycamore tree. He chewed on something with his big yellow teeth, the one bucking fang foremost amongst its peers and doing the honorary piercing of the flesh of whatever it was being eaten. Drool would leak from the lower lip crowned by that great tooth, a sad mouth that could never fully close. Having stopped to stare, Tilly slowly raised her arm to greet the strange child with a wave.

The child ignored her, and kept chewing.

"Who are you, bucktooth?" Willy shouted without hesitation. "Never seen you round here before!" But the child did not reply.

"That was mean," said Billy, "we don't even know him. Maybe he's not right in the head."

"We could call him Buck if that makes you feel better. Doesn't look like he'll be giving us his name anyhow."

The three just lucked at Buck, chewing away his hours.

"What in tarnations is he chewin' on?"

Tilly asked the question but nudged Willy to be the one taking a closer look, which he refused with mounting unease, until the other two pressed Willy with heavy accusatory looks. He stepped closer to Buck, who kept chewing away without a care. Willy became more horrified the closer he got; having got a clearer view of the strange child, it became more obvious there was something wrong with the boy; he smelled like death, like it had crawled out of the ground not realizing it should not have been capable of moving at all.

Yet, Willy could see the boy's chest rise and fall, and hear the shallow breathing over the sound of chewing. The boy also had red stains on his hands and Willy gasped, feeling dizzy and unable to walk back. This had to be some sort of ghoul, or mountain spirit; a haint as the locals called all matter of terrible creatures that came down from the surrounding mountains, or from under the hills to roam the woods and fields that were all about them. Everyone was familiar with the cackling of witches, the meowling of the human-faced cats and the attacks of the skin shedders every full moon. This felt different, somehow.

Bucky moved his hands then, as he made to bite deeper into what he was chewing and what he was eating became visible to Willy, who managed to exhale in relief before turning to the others.

"He's just eating a tomato!" Willy moved around the boy and found a pile of discarded skins, seeds and other refuge. "Oh man, that's a lot! I think we should change his name to Tom!"

"Tom what?" Tilly could see the joke coming faster than a speeding train and rolled her eyes and huffed before Billy got his answer from Willy.

"Tom Ater!" Willy shouted and guffawed, slapping his thighs and turning red from laughing so hard he cried a little, looking like a tomato himself. All three of them circled the boy now, who finished eating his tomato with hands and mouth dirty with tomato pulp and they wondered how long the boy had been there, or even where he had come from.

"Hey. Hey! Where did you come from?" Willy had his hands on his knees and leaned close to Bucky so he could see him eye to eye. He repeated again slowly "Where are you from?"

Bucky simply looked him in the eyes without replying though it was somewhat questionable if he was even seeing Willy, or looking past him. Bucky's eyes were truly alien, black pools that could as well be blind. This made Billy nervous so he lashed out and pushed the boy who fell to his side but didn't speak or move to defend himself, instead looking up dumbly as he turned to face the trio.

"You think you're too good to talk to us? You haint? Run back to your hole!"

Bucky didn't react, his breathing was the same and didn't even blink. Tilly realized she hadn't seen him blink once, so maybe he didn't even need to blink at all, unless he did it when she did it. Willy became more agitated by the lack of reaction from the boy, and feeling emboldened by Bucky's lack of reaction from Billy's abuse, he picked a clump of dirt and threw it at Bucky.

Nothing. He got another handful of dirt and mud, then another and Billy joined him in unleashing a barrage of such clumps. They became so many and hit with such force that Bucky had to eventually try to shield himself with his arms. The two boys jeered and yelled, and Tilly felt half tempted to join as she had realized that Bucky wasn't right and that, at least in her eyes, it wasn't a sickness or that he was dumb but rather that he wasn't human.

His tooth as well as something behind those strange eyes made her realize it. As Bucky finally made to stand up and run, Tilly saw that even his fingers were different. They were webbed with a flap of skin that went up to his knuckles; not only that but also his arms and legs were skinny and arched weirdly, with tufts of black hair here and there. She walked backwards and half expected to see Bucky howl and call to him a bunch of wolf people to come to his aid but the boy stumbled off, tumbling down and standing back up clumsily in his slow escape.

Bucky was covered with dirt and blood, his own blood dark as molasses. The boys started throwing rocks mixed with clumps of dirt they picked up, and Tilly could guess how much that hurt and bruised. Bucky would be covered in wounds. His dirty clothes were filthy and torn, more so than before. As he fled, the boys gave chase and Tilly stood where she was, shouting at them to stop, begging them to turn back.

They ignored her completely and went after Bucky across the fields and into the woods forcing her to make a split-second choice. Would she go all the way back to try and get an adult or chase after them? Whatever Bucky was, or how scared he made her feel, he had done nothing wrong. Maybe he stole the tomatoes he had been eating but that had done her no harm and was none of her business. If this kept up the boys might end up killing Bucky just for fun and that felt wrong; worst yet, she would be too late if she tried to go get help, adults having no more power than her when it came to undoing death.

She started chasing after the boys, passing by farmable land, sometimes trampling on it until they reached the edge of the woods. Her friends were still chasing the boy, and Tilly only stopped at the very threshold to try and recover her breath as they disappeared into the wild.

Once out of sight, the only sign of them was the sound of their screaming and running through that waning piece of an old world that modern life consumed with unending appetite for hundreds of years and would continue to do so until it was all gone. For the time being it was all there still, an alien world full of unknown things that scared her, and though she couldn't put it into words she knew by instinct to be afraid to step in and risk herself to be taken.

Her ears could barely capture the sounds as they grew more distant and the woods swallowed all. She stepped past the tree line, slowly, afraid of getting lost more than of losing them so she walked in but stopped again as panic took hold. Those paths between the trees grew darker, forming tunnels in a maze of wood, grass and dirt. They made her dizzy until she couldn't take it and had to turn back.

Tilly left the woods without regrets, heading home all by herself to let it all go on without her. After all, none of it was her problem.

***

The boys were having the time of their lives, jumping and racing wildly after the freak. They couldn't contain their excitement, a crave for a violence they had not even imagined but were eager to find a way to shape. Having lost track of time, and with Tilly completely forgotten as well, nothing stopped them from going deeper and deeper out into a stretch of the wood that was empty, deadly quiet and no sign of Bucky. They looked around, sweaty and breathless.

Where was the little freak? He was nowhere to be seen. Only when both boys stopped long enough to look around them, they realized they didn't know where they were or how to get back. Willy didn't panic, possessed with the certainty only the most careless young can muster. Death was something foreign to them, and so all would sort itself with enough time, as if by magic. Something moved in the bush, close enough to be heard but with enough stealth that it remained unseen.

Willy sprinted after the sound and Billy followed, again and again, chasing. Hours had passed and it had gotten terribly dark. Billy cracked first.

"Let's go back, I don't want to do this anymore." His friend ignored him completely, trapped in his own frustration.

"Where are you! Get out here and let me see you!" But as much as he tried, shouting as loudly as he could, nothing answered. Willy wouldn't have been able to explain why he had expected a reply from a boy that had, so far, appeared to be mute.

Both boys stood silent for a long dragging moment and past the breeze rustling the leaves, the cicadas and the sound of their own ragged breathing there was something else, like a whisper. With no other means, truly lost now with barely any moonlight to show them their path they followed that sound which became clearer as they drew nearer.

A spring, on a small clearing and decorated by the world's smallest waterfall. Sweet fresh water, the white foam and bubble of it falling into the pond it formed under the cascade, splashing from moss covered rocks as it flowed down. It reminded them immediately of how thirsty they were and also how that was a warm night, one made warmer by all their running. They kneeled by the water and ran deep into it, without dreaming how deep the pond went.

It was a natural well and at the bottom, and deep beneath it was that same water running underground through tunnels of soil, deep mud full of secrets.

Bucky was behind them and all he had to do was push.

They never heard him coming and they splashed in the water in a panic, breathing in some of the water as Bucky jumped after them, biting with his long tooth.

Bucky tore at their necks, hands and forearms as they tried to stay afloat and push him off. Willy sank as Bucky, who was only strong enough to pull one of the boys down, pushed and dragged in turn to the muddy depths, his helpless once upon a time bully.

Billy managed to drag himself out of the water, sore from screaming for his life and stumbled out back into the woods. He tripped barely twelve steps out, and fell flat on his face. He looked up, crying and speechless as dark humanoid shapes glided down from the tree branches to meet him, their oversized teeth reflecting a stray beam of moonlight that had finally managed to break through a cloudy sky and the all-encompassing embrace of the tree branches.

Before the night was over, the two boys were reunited, buried together in the mud, the dirt seeping into the cuts on their skin.

***

Tilly avoided the usual route for months. Whenever asked about the boys she would just say she had seen them run into the woods and had been too scared, and too tired to follow. Not once did she make mention of Buck; of all things she had learned to fear, she feared what meeting others like Buck would do to the families who tried to chase these neighbors. Despite having not delved into the woods like the boys did, she had seen enough haints to know these strange neighbors were never alone on their own.

She had told her parents about her missing friends, and her parents told the others but though the adults scoured those woods never finding signs and eventually losing hope, and she grew all the more lonely for the other local children, never cared to approach her as if suspecting the trio had gone too far their antics, perhaps blaming her or worse finding her to be a coward having doomed the boys in her weakness to follow after them, or warned their parents of the boy's antics when there had been time to do something.

Whatever was said of her behind her back, as unfair as it was to blame a child for something so terrible and as lonely and upset as she was, she mostly just felt tired. The day came when Tilly had not even realized she had taken back to the route she used to walk with the boys, and as she reached that tree under which she had seen Buck, she felt her breath getting trapped in her lungs.

Three forms sat under the tree, eating fruit, three gray skinned boys with jaundiced eyes and vacant stares. Dressed in dirty and torn clothes. Familiar clothes she could never forget. Tilly stopped, separated from them by the small distance and the fence, and she stared at how they had changed. Willy had swollen like he had drowned and then been turned and Billy's head looked wrong, dented, and one of his eyes was missing. All three had a few teeth between them grown too big for their mouths, buck teeth that they used to bite into handful after handful of strawberries. Their eyes met Tilly's but there was no recognition behind them.

Tilly cried in silence, turned away from them and kept walking back home. She never told another soul of what she saw, nor did she ever walk that path again.

BETTER TO KILL THE STORK

Monica loved to dance, experiencing the freedom and joy of life condensed into an art form. She felt she could express herself to the sound of something bigger than herself; the beating heart of existence itself marked the rhythm of her movements. Life had been rough, but music and dance took it all away. This had been just another night out on the town, free and careless, until Monica saw him.

She was only sixteen, while he must have been at least twenty-something. Under the lights and the deafening music, his face. The way he moved through the crowd, he had been to her a beacon ready to guide her out of a stormy sea. She shouldn't have gone to him, but she did. He should have told her to get away from him, but he didn't

The sex was good, and the regret was absent until months later, when she found out she was pregnant. She couldn't have the abortion without her parent's permission.

"Please, please, I don't want this! I'll be more careful, but I need you now!"

"You need to face what you did. How would you have felt if I had done it? If I had gotten rid of you?"

"That doesn't even make sense!" Monica cried, her face hot with anger. The combination of her mother's betrayal and the frustration from Monica's impotence to rescue herself were too much for any person to bear. "Mother! Please, you can't make me do this!"

"You'll do what you're told! You'll carry this child and thank me and your father for not kicking you out!"

Monica looked to her father, who said nothing. Always the coward, he couldn't even look her in the eye. It was as if the birth of a child Monica didn't want wasn't his problem. This, a life changing event that would impact everyone who was part of Monica's life. How could he turn his back to something like this, to leave Monica who was his own child, to stand alone against such a storm?

He looked away while Monica's mother continued to tell her everything she thought right, what she thought was fair for her daughter and the coming grandchild.

***

Months passed every day, a nightmare. Monica couldn't believe her child was real when she finally held the baby in her arms. She knew she was holding a breathing, living thing but no matter how hard she tried she didn't love *it*. All the months of pain, of losing time she would never recover, had been just steps to be on that hospital bed, holding the child in her arms and she couldn't even think of the child as a person. Her parents had made it into a *thing*, a life changing burden.

"I don't want you." It was dark, maybe 3:00 A.M. and Monica had been left alone with the baby, a girl she hadn't even named yet. "The way they looked at me when I said I didn't know who your father was. How I hadn't picked a name for you. I never wanted any of this."

Monica gently rested the baby girl back on the crib next to her bed. "I don't hate you, but I don't love you." She looked at the sleeping child, understanding without ever admitting to anyone - not even herself - that she was still a child as well, though she didn't feel like one anymore.

Her parents had brought a few things on their visit, including clothes for her and the baby. She stood up, and nearly fell from being weakened by a difficult birth. Despite hurting and feeling faint, she managed to get herself dressed while making as little noise as possible. Monica didn't look back, afraid she would change her mind.

They had kept her long enough that she knew every corridor, as well as the routines of the nurses. Ironically, the staff had advised the parents to consider a abortion to prevent the risks of a potential miscarriage. Fate had other plans however, or at least her mother did. Long weeks followed, hope was given and then taken; a thousand procedures were performed like habits until they became as natural as waking up. Yes, Monica had come to know the walls and wills of her prison well.

No one would stop her, most of the staff was gone or busy at this time and the old nurse guarding the maternity ward would be busy somewhere or simply fast asleep at her station.

Knowing she didn't have enough money to last her beyond a bus ticket and some meals, Monica felt tempted to steal something on her way out. It was too risky so she focused on escaping; to stay, or to be found out would be a death sentence.

Despite not actually being deserted, the hospital felt empty. At night the corridors looked strange to her. Even with directions written on the walls, Monica felt like she was trying to reach the end of a labyrinth in a nightmare.

A pain in her chest weighed her down, greater than the soreness of her abdomen and legs. She stopped by a vending machine, the light a beacon. Its humming was the only thing cutting the silence, until she heard another sound.

Her back stiffened. Whispers chased her from dark corners, places she had traveled and previously found empty. Monica heard the whispers grow louder but could not discern any words. Then came a third sound, something fleshy slapping against tiled floors.

Monica held her breath. She walked backwards with her eyes fixed at the end of the corridor she had come from as the sound became louder to the point of echoing in those big empty halls, until it stopped. It felt as if Monica's heart had stopped along with it.

Nothing came. Nothing happened but as she exhaled, she heard it breathe. It was a raspy, half-whistled noise. She looked down and illuminated by the glow of the vending machine she saw something that looked like a worm laying still on the ground.

It moved when she took a step back. From a corner appeared part of a small face, an eye that peeked at Monica. It stared at her with its single swollen eye.

Monica covered her mouth with both her hands, nails digging to the sides of her face, every muscle in her body tensed. A pain in her abdomen bloomed like a forest of thorns. Locked up in her terror, she may have reopened some wounds, but she didn't dare cry for help. Instead, she turned to limp away awkwardly, stumbling for her life.

Arrows with directions on the corridor walls had text that blurred as Monica struggled to stay awake, blood dripping down her legs. Every door seemed to be locked or leading to a room too dark to see. Every window reflected her ashen, panic-stricken face. She was drenched in sweat, her hair like a swimmer's, many a strand of it glued to her forehead.

Monica stopped again, her pursuer tirelessly drawing nearer, crawling and dragging behind it a body she did not want to imagine. Facing her was a door leading to a stairwell, and a way down: a back exit that would let her reach the ground floor. She didn't have her clothes, not even a pair of slippers to shield the soles of her feet, but she would get herself on the ground outside, even if it meant suffering a thousand cuts.

She had to reach the ground floor in order to escape and this was the way to go. With no time to waste, she opened the door for the emergency exit. Monica slowly made her way down the stairs, too weak and hurt to run, and too scared of slipping and hurting herself.

Half a flight of stairs down, she realized something was wrong. The stairs never seemed to end; steps appeared after every step, making her spiral endlessly. She sat on a step and tried to recover her breath. Monica realized she had not left the building at all. Somehow, she had been turned around, and so she told herself, going up and down the stairs like an idiot.

The stress, exhaustion, and drugs must have combined to confuse her, even if the pain signaled to her brain that the drugs must have worn off. Monica even dared to tell herself nothing was chasing but that was when she heard it.

It *cooed*.

It plopped heavily down the steps, slowly making its way towards her. It had grown, and she saw its lumpy body was almost as big as she was and it dragged itself with its swollen arms. It drooled from the corners of its misshapen mouth, its huge head tilted sideways. Its eyelids were swollen, but it managed to open its eyes enough to reveal the dark wet pools underneath. They were dark mirrors in which

Monica saw her own reflection. In horror she stood up again and ran. The monster followed, calling for her with the parody of child-like noises. Monica slammed against a door to her left, an emergency exit and stepped outside, into the night.

She found a parking lot and ran for it, rushing past the facility's small garden.

The door slammed open again behind her as ran. The thing made sounds of frustration that neared on squeals. She hadn't planned for this, for obvious reasons. Even without this thing chasing her Monica would have been forced to improvise at this point.

She wasn't far from the street, but her body was giving up on her, her mind reeling at what chased her. Anything further than arm's length began to blur. The cars under the streetlights were little more than shiny blurs themselves.

"What's going on?" Someone had come out of one of the cars, the headlights on and the motor still running. Monica couldn't make out any features on this stranger. The voice sounded male. She latched on to this person and screamed for help.

"What?"

They couldn't say much else as they stared in terror. It was the monster, the child now as big as one of the cars, crying angrily and pushing itself towards them. Monica couldn't afford the time to to waste any time, she jumped in the car, taking the driver's seat.

The stranger only had time to turn and open his mouth when the child pounced on him. It began to tear with blind fury at the man whose screams died quickly, muffled as they were by the immensity of the monster. Then the former car owner was torn apart by those grotesque and inept malformed hands. Monica took off, and the misshapen head turned awkwardly to watch her go. With one blood-drenched hand, still holding to the gristle and torn clothes of the man it had slaughtered, the babe reached in vain.

Monica stopped some distance away, trying to regain her sight before driving toward the busy streets . From the rearview mirror, she saw the reflection of the child quickly stumbling towards her. I tried to stand on two legs and failed. The ground under her wheels shook ,and the thing went back to crawling on all fours, staring at her with its massive eyes.

Monica hadn't gotten her driver's license, but she had some experience driving her father's car. She thought about what her escape would look like and she thought perhaps, this was her chance. If she backed over the thing with this car she could hurt it, maybe even kill it.

It couldn't be her baby; it couldn't be. Monica was normal and the child had been born normal. But what if it was her child? Monica couldn't put her feelings into words. how divided she felt, or why she cared.

It was getting closer. Her time was running out. Ahead of her, the road was empty. There wasn't another soul in this sight. If any godlike being was watching, it was doing so mockingly. A horrid parent, full of disdain for all of the children of creation.

No one cared for Monica but herself. So, she did what she had to do, the thing inches from catching up. She drove forward, leaving it behind, growing more and more distant. It tried to give chase, but the car was too fast, and Monica sped toward her freedom. She felt faint and ignored it, only slowing down hours later. She was still unsure if she had headed the right way.

Monica prayed that she could stay awake until she crossed some sort of border, too far away by the laws of man to get sent back. Just one more mile, and she could start again.

Just one more mile.

Just one more mile.

Just one more mile.

Just one more...

MY FRIEND SCOTT

Recording for the Paulo Meneses case. This is Emma da Cruz, ID 19122022.

The following is an audio reproduction, made in accordance with the current procedures for improving accessibility and conserving records for ongoing cases. I will be reading from the school work assignment submitted in 2002, by a student of St. Lucia's Primary School on the day of their disappearance. The parents were interviewed multiple times and when questioned regarding the contents of the following document, they have always refused to comment.

There have been no leads aside from the assignment itself and the crude drawing that accompanies it. The assignment text reads as follows:

My name is Paulo and my best friend is called Scott.

I call him Scott because he has black fur like Scott had before he had to go to a farm. My friend Scott has a very long face and big eyes. His eyes are brown, like mine, and I talk to him a lot. Scott doesn't talk back, but he looks at me and pays a lot of attention when I'm talking.

He's very nice and sits by my bed at night to hear me when I talk to him. Sometimes it's very dark but I know he's there because I can see his eyes and they look a little shiny.

He never talks or barks or growls. He's very good and listens to me talk and if there's a storm outside or a big ambulance noise, he shows his teeth which means he's scared.

*Sometimes he's somewhere else in the house but I can hear him because he goes **tap, tap, tap!** If he runs, he goes like this:*

TAPTAPTAPTAPTAPTAP

Because he has long nails that are very round and they hit the floor when he walks and it sounds like he's making a little dance.

Mommy said it's the rats but I told her it was Scott, and she didn't like it and was very angry at me. She doesn't believe me and always says I shouldn't lie or be mean but I wasn't. I know it's Scott.

She said daddy would be home soon but he wasn't, that night and the night before he came home very late. I know because I woke up and Scott was sitting next to my bed looking at the door and I could see his teeth because daddy was very loud and loud noises made Scott scared.

I drew a lot of pictures of Scott and me but mommy didn't like it. She showed them to daddy and they both told me to stop. It's okay because I don't want to show them more until I get really good. My teacher said I could leave the drawings with the other ones I make in her class. She said "practice makes perfect" and I think when I draw it perfect, they'll believe me. I think she doesn't like my drawings but she's very nice and tells me to keep drawing so I like her.

Scott has a very long face, big eyes like a person and big ears. Really big. I can't see him sometimes when everything is black like he is. He walks on four legs but I saw him standing up one time.

I can go home from the school bus stop all on my own now, and that's how we met; he followed me home the day I got tired and stopped by a big tree. There's lots and lots of trees, and the leaves were all brown. I saw him standing on two legs and I was scared, because I couldn't see him well and thought he was a bear but he wasn't.

He got very close and was looking down at me. I looked up and said "Hello, my name is Paulo" and he didn't say anything because he doesn't talk but he turned his head to the side like Scott does, when I say a thing and he wants to understand. He's a smart dog and I miss him.

That's why I called my new friend Scott.

When he got home with me, I was afraid mommy would be scared but she never saw him. I gave him some of my food but he never ate anything I gave him.

I tried meatloaf, fish sticks, cookies with chocolate chips, and a carrot.

*He likes to play fetch so when I am told to go play outside, I throw sticks for him to catch. Sometimes I run and he runs after me and because we're outside on the grass I don't hear him go **tap tap** or **TAPTAPTAP** anymore. Instead, he goes **shshshshshshsh** and when he catches me, he puts his face very close to mine. I laugh because he looks silly.*

Yesterday I scraped my knee because I was running again and I fell and there was a rock. There was blood on my knee, it was my right knee and he licked it and it tickled. When I showed my knee to mommy, she was worried and her face looked funny but she put that thing that burns to make it better.

When I woke up this morning Scott wasn't there. I was worried but today during the first recess I heard him *go **shshshsh** in the grass. During English class with teacher Mr. Muniz who is a little mean because he always tells me I'm very slow. I always tell him I'm slow because I want to write perfectly so everyone understands me but he doesn't believe me and says everyone else writes better and faster and that I can't be so slow.*

*It makes me want to cry, but he went away now to be mean to Lucinda who sits behind me in class and I can hear Scott **tap tap tap** in the corridor.*

I bet Scott is worried about me too, so I think I should go find him and say hi and give him a hug so he knows I'm okay and I'm going to show him one of the drawings I made today.

I think I got really good because this one really looks like him.

Due to lack of evidence, and no other apparent sightings in the past ten years of either Paulo, or whoever took him, the case will be archived. I am forced to apply a classification to the case and hereby make it clear I do not agree with this aspect of the procedure, and I'm doing so against my will, since I believe there are insufficient grounds to apply a definitive classification. Since the privatization, we've been pushed further to reduce the number of unsolved or cold cases, for no other reason than to meet quotas imposed by investors.

I was instructed, upon consulting with a superior, to archive this under Animal Attack and will do so, while Paulo will be classified as Assumed as Deceased.

Sadly, I may have to agree with the latter.

HIGH STRUNG

Lewis had never been happy. You may wonder what a boy knows at age fifteen. You may question also: if such a boy had never known happiness, how could he know it was an absent thing in his life?

It was a simple matter of observation. Even if he attempted to fake the emotion, he couldn't. Others were able to find joy, to live and love while Lewis couldn't.

He judged his life as normal, more or less. His parents were loving. He got along well enough with others, despite himself. It was just that feeling of being empty that haunted him. If you have ever looked away at nothing for long minutes before realizing what you were doing and stopping yourself, then you know a little of what it is like to be Lewis.

The absence of joy was like this for him. It was not really a present sadness but just a numbness. Being Lewis was the equivalent of living inside a movie theater, seeing people in the images projected against a flat surface.

Light and sound were distant things as he sat in the dark, every chair around him empty. His notions of what life was like came through those images, those sounds. Distant. Beyond his reach. Things that happened in the movie couldn't happen to him.

Some people who knew Lewis were perceptive enough to tell something wasn't quite right with the boy. They weren't cruel about it; they wouldn't pick on him, or tease him but neither did they deal with his problems. It was common practice to assume that there are things people have to solve on their own, and Lewis had a mess no one else wanted to get mixed up in.

***

"Let's go to Busted High!"

"Banhart? It's just homeless people sleeping there now."

"There's a ghost! We should go find it."

Steven laughed, and Liz pushed him a bit. Doug and Marta found the idea of visiting the old building irresistible, and started talking about what to tell their parents in order to circumvent curfew.

"We don't need to stay up too late. Someone from another class said they saw something on their way home from school, so we just need to be there around that time and try to get a look inside."

"What did they see?"

"A ghost peeking out of a window!"

"Ah ah! Let me guess, was it Sad Seymour?"

"I don't know, she didn't ask the ghost's name."

"Hey, Lewis! What do you think, wanna come along and ask the ghost's name?"

"I don't believe in ghosts?"

"Aww, don't be boring! Come on, it will be fun!"

"Why did he say it like a question?"

"Yeah, come along! I bet it's Sad Seymour!"

"Who's Sad Seymour?"

The bell rang and Lewis's friends didn't get a chance to tell him then. Once classes were done, they got him to tag along so they could correct that.

"There was a teacher who killed himself. All the kids used to make fun of him and then one day a janitor found Seymour hanging from the classroom ceiling."

"Sometimes people say they saw his ghost peeking from a window and they always say it's him because his neck is all messed up."

"That sounds awful. You guys really want to go there?"

"I don't believe any of it, but it's not like we have anything better to do today."

"The ghost is super real!"

"Aw, come on!"

They all laughed, except Lewis. He couldn't even make himself fake a smile for this one, feeling sorry for the teacher who had been mocked in life and continued to be made fun of in death.

"Why did people make fun of him back then?"

"I don't know man; we make fun of most of our teachers so it was probably the same back then."

"I heard he looked weird."

"I heard he killed his mother!"

"Jeez, Liz! What the hell?"

"What? It's what I heard! Beth and Wanda were the ones who told me."

The sun started to set behind the old building. The old rusty gates were found wide open to allow them in. Lewis didn't notice who ran in first because he got distracted looking at the ruin.

There was a broken window, and some crude drawings done with spray paint. None of them knew how empty the place had become.

He imagined that at night, when the shadows hid the damage time had done to the building, it probably looked the same as his current school.

Lewis looked and saw something on one of the floors. It was too blurry to make out, and it vanished when his friends called him.

"Come on, Lewis!"

He followed, and they circled the school building first. There was an old gym on the back of the school, to the right of it. They tried to get in but it was too well locked up.

"Guess we're drinking outside."

Lewis hadn't even realized they had brought beer. He was handed one and drank, not particularly caring for the taste but having enough practice to drink it so he could integrate a little better.

He only took small sips, and never had more than one beer because the idea made him nervous. He saw how much everyone started talking, the things they would say and Lewis didn't trust himself to open up and not regret it.

It was fun. Everyone had a good time talking, singing and drinking. All he had to do was to stay sober enough not to say something stupid, something he couldn't take back.

"Ever seen a ghost before?"

Marta had asked the question. She was on her third beer by the time he had drunk about a third of his first and only.

"No. I don't think so. How about you?"

She always had so much energy, which made the usually demure Lewis feel jealous. Now she was leaning on him and looking up at the sky that had started to fill with stars.

"I think I saw my mom once."

Lewis clamped up, fighting back the *I'm sorry*, that wanted to escape his lips. She didn't want his apologies and didn't need his pity;

the others were too busy being loud and she had trusted him with something personal, because she wanted to be heard.

"When?"

"A year after she died, I was nine. I woke one night and I saw her at the foot of my bed."

Lewis looked at her, but her eyes stayed focused on the sky. They were silent for a moment, letting the sound of the wind and the noise being made by the others fill that space.

"Did she say something to you?"

Marta shook her head.

"No, I think I remember her smiling at me and then I fell asleep. It was like blinking. And then it was morning, so maybe it was a dream... but it felt real. I really wanted it to be real."

They both drank from their beers.

"Have you tried seeing her again?"

"Yeah. I played all those games for calling up ghosts but nothing ever happened."

Silence, for just a moment before all the noise returned.

"You think we'll see a ghost tonight?"

Marta sat straight and nudged him a bit with her elbow.

"You ask a lot of questions! How about you tell me this: do you want to see a ghost?"

Lewis didn't hesitate.

"No. At least I hope we don't see the one you guys were talking about. I just want to hang out and then go home before my parents figure out I've been drinking and turn *me* into a ghost."

"Jeez, are they that serious? You never drink at all."

They weren't that serious.

"Oh yeah, they would be super pissed at me. That's why I only drink one, and they won't notice. How about your dad?"

Marta shrugged it off. "If he finds out he finds out. Never got in trouble before."

She did seem to be the one from their friend group who could drink the most without sounding drunk, and though Lewis had never thought about it before, it probably helped avoid getting in trouble when she got back home.

They walked the corridors of the abandoned school building. Though no one said it, they all felt the strange sense of familiarity as this school was much like their own. They were walking on the ghost of their school, a grave for their own future, not knowing their own school would one day be like this; just another abandoned and broken building.

What they could feel was that this was wrong. Disorienting. Why were the schools built so much alike?

Time was the first thing they lost in the dark halls, their phones illuminating empty class rooms with piled up broken chairs and other rubble. What they lost next was their patience.

"Let's split up! I made a chat group on UpDog so the first of us to see a ghost can call using the app and share a video with everyone."

Lewis couldn't remember if Doug had always been this proactive and practical before. He wondered how much his friend was into ghost hunting. Though Steven had been the one to suggest it, maybe the other boy had been the one to plant the idea.

They formed their groups and Liz seemed to make a move for Lewis before being pulled by the other girls in a wild run down one of the stairways, screaming and laughing as children are prone to do. Being quiet and not particularly interested in finding ghosts, Lewis ended up drifting on his own going up another flight of stairs.

He found a blocked corridor to his right, full of broken-down book cases, desks and tables. Turning left he walked past broken and dirty windows looking outside. Their little town was all lit up now like a Christmas tree. The sound of distant speeding cars came up carried by the breeze, along with the rustling of tree branches, one of which had grown into one of the broken windows for some reason.

Plants reached towards the light, not the other way around. It was odd and the branch made for strange shadows. It scratched the ceiling of the classroom and creaked like old furniture as the wind made it move like an arm, with long talons. Lewis stared at the thing but soon made to leave.

It creaked again as Lewis turned, but different, louder, as if moved by a weight. Followed by a wheeze. The young man stopped on his tracks, waited to hear silence, but instead there was another creak and wheeze..

And the weeping.

Lewis took some deep breaths, readying himself. He had to see, or be sure there was nothing to see. So he turned, and facing him was a body hanging from the tree branch. The face had become so distended and swollen it could hardly read as a face, but instead as the parody of one.

The neck also seemed long, twisted at strange angles.

The rest was human enough, a man in a disheveled shirt and old suit pants, kneeling pathetically on the ground. The branch and the length of his neck made it so he couldn't really hang from it. Wet shapes, the ghost's eyes rolled to stare in the boy's direction.

Usually the teenager didn't feel much, yet for the second or third time that night something pierced the numbness of life. The figure was strange and revolting but what lingering fear he may have felt, Lewis could now only feel pity for the ghost.

"Hello?"

He greeted the spirit but it did not reply, at least not with words. These appear to be beyond the apparition's powers. It swung and spun slowly from the branch it was hanging from. Its eyes locked onto the young man's eyes.

Lewis was terrified again, fearing this was all an act to lure him into a trap. What would happen if he got too close, or the thing touched him? He walked away backwards, out of the room. The spirit moaned in pain, as if begging for Lewis to return. Lewis looked, making sure he wouldn't trip on something. He was all the way down the corridor when he stopped to see if the phantom had chased him.

All that followed were the moans. Rather than to go find the others, Lewis returned to the classroom. Again, the ghost locked eyes with him, as if it could not move anything other than its eyes.

"If you can understand me, blink once."

Slowly, the ghost blinked once and after it kept its eyes wide open. They had a terror to them that failed to reach the rest of its limp face.

"Do you want me to help you down?"

It blinked again, just once and it kept its eyes open, as some substance trickled down the corners of its eyes like tears.

Lewis fought against his instinct to run away and approached the ghost. He took a good look at the rope and could not figure out how to undo the knot. The branch looked solid but if it couldn't break, maybe it could bend enough that Lewis could slip out the rope.

Lewis tugged at the rope, putting his weight into pulling it. The ghost's limp form slushed against the floor, the wet noise it made as that sagged and distended body laid further on the old floor made him cringe. It was as if the ghost's body was full of liquid, the skin nothing but a rubber to keep the wet contents inside.

Lewis pulled harder and something snapped, throwing him back. He tried to sit up, hoping the noise would not bring in the others. The branch stood as before, intact, but the rope was broken in two, and the ghost was motionless on the ground, its body torn as well and oozing something vile.

It wheezed a sigh of what Lewis hoped was relief and as the wet contents poured out began to evaporate. The ghost itself began to crumble, falling apart and becoming dust.

"What the fuck!?"

Lewis turned to see Marta framed against the door. He said nothing, lost for words he stood up and Marta came to him. She let Lewis lean on her and they both stared at the floor and the spreading stain.

From where the ghost's form had crumpled, the dust dissolved into the puddle and from it flew a small shape. To them it looked like an insect, a moth perhaps. It took flight and escaped out the window, perhaps guided by moonlight.

***

No one else saw anything.

General disappointment was quickly subdued by the pleasant buzz of alcohol doing its job to cushion the fall. No one seemed to notice the drenched Lewis.

"Man, I hope at least that smell washes off."

Marta was very nonchalant about their encounter with a spirit, and Lewis played along as best he could.

"I think I'll just throw away the clothes."

Marta leaned closer, and talked in a half whisper.

"So, like... We turn into moths when we die?"

Lewis didn't know how to react, his whole body tensed until she started laughing. It was the saddest laugh he had ever heard, so full of life but so desperate to break something loose, to give some meaning to the shapeless chaos that pulled them to its center.

He joined in. It felt good to laugh out loud, and to do so in the company of others. For the first time he could recall, there was comfort instead of awkwardness and he laughed even louder; loud enough to muffle the fluttering of little wings.

Last Call to Casas

The weather was burning hot. The sun's rays were amplified by the pollutants that seeped into the very air, unseen, but with effects that were felt. Inside the tall, modern building in midtown however, it was freezing cold. He had looked up to the familiar name and the large icon that was both religious symbol and brand logo. Leonardo Casas wondered if this was what the savior had died for. Despite the hypocrisy of it all, he had still walked in with some hope left.

"The program is called New Homes for the New World. We can guarantee the child will do immensely well. All the parents went through a rigorous process so we know they are the best fit for the program."

Leonardo felt his frail hope crumble. These were the white lies told by people with perfect white teeth, wearing their expensive clothes and sitting behind their custom-made desks in fancy office buildings.

"I see." Leonardo lied in return, looking the woman from the adoption agency in the eyes. She didn't seem to blink. Ever. "I wouldn't be doing something like this if I could prevent it. I love my son and I want that to be clear."

"Of course, we would never –"

"I'm sick. Like my wife was. I can't afford both treatment and looking after him, not at the same time. I got paid some small compensation for her death, but my health is getting worse. I need to... I want to see my son again."

She waited, with her unblinking eyes and static smile, and resumed her assurances when she was sure he would not interrupt her.

"I'm sure the Lord will guide you to a quick recovery. As I was saying, the parents are good people. We pick only the best; these are familiar names and faces from our congregation. Respectful, good souls who could not be blessed with children otherwise. Your son will be lucky no matter who adopts him, because he will be loved."

"Right." Leonardo pushed back the start of a coughing fit, "and if I want to see my son again?"

"Oh, it can be arranged. Naturally, the parents will have to be informed first."

"Adoptive parents."

"Yes, that's what I meant."

He looked at her, but the woman smiled back and added nothing more to it.

"Is there anything I should know before I agree to any of this?"

"It's all in the papers, Mr. Casas. I would be happy to go over them again with you."

"Thank you. Since you offered, I do have some questions about the fine print." He waited to see how she would react while he turned the pages one by one, trying to upset her, to get a reaction that hinted at her being a human being like him. She did not react, her smile unflinching. For a moment he imagined her face was a mask, and that nothing existed behind the polite facade, nothing but a void.

"Here." He pointed at a particularly long paragraph and turned it to her; the woman's eyes moved, angling down and reading the words.

She never moved her head. "This makes it look like I give up all visiting rights, which doesn't really add up with what you said."

"It's just for an initial period; we want the children to acclimate to their new home. Build routines with their new family. You will be able to visit Antonio any time, that is, within reason."

Despite the cold air, Leonardo felt his chest burning hot. The heat spread upwards, bringing with a dizziness that made him hold to the armrests of the chair, while the woman facing him contorted grotesquely. In his delirium, she looked like a wax figure, carved into a disdainful effigy, moving stiffly.

"Mr. Casas?"

"What do you mean within reason?"

"Naturally we don't want to tax the family..."

"I'm the family!" Leonardo was too loud, the words escaping him before he managed to get a hold of himself. He swallowed dry a few times and tried to regain control before talking again; Leonardo could only push so far without getting kicked out.

"Maria and I gave everything we could to the congregation; we worked as hard as everyone else and never missed mass. My son is all the family I have left, and I was told to trust the congregation like we always have, for years. Our minister says we're all equal in the eyes of God, but it doesn't feel like it right now. Not with me sitting here, and you – I mean the congregation, not really telling me anything."

"It's all in the papers, Mr. Casas."

"No, it really isn't. No names, no visiting hours, no one to talk about it outside of the congregation and no time to think it through." He pointed at the paperwork. "These, your papers, phrase it all so vaguely it feels like I'm agreeing to a kidnapping."

Again, her eyes remained unblinking, dead, but the woman's smile became a scowl as she leaned forward, her fingers steepled.

"Mister Casas. I have spoken with many parents, and will have to speak with many more before the day is over. Some of the parents coming to us are not as fortunate as you are; they beg to us for help. They beg us, Mr. Casas. For my colleagues and I to rescue their children from poverty. Unlike your son, not every child is blessed to have such luck as to be taken in by these loving couples we painstakingly select."

Her voice was cold and artificial, like the air they were breathing. Even in a moment of apparent anger, it was all rehearsed. That felt wrong and upsetting to Leonardo.

"Your wife was sick, you are sick, and your child could be next. God sent us harsh punishments, but it is for the children we run these programs, to rescue their innocent souls. We feel terribly sorry for your situation, Mister Casas, but in this we are like Noah; there's not enough room in the ark for everyone." She held a hand up to silence him, reading him like a book, knowing he meant to cut her off. He would have ignored her command, but it was hard to hold back another coughing fit. Leonardo swallowed back his disgust, and his powerlessness to stand up against the powers that be.

"These are healthy, God-fearing couples. One such couple wants your child. If they could, they would adopt all the children, but they can't. It would also be unfair to them to make them accept a child that is sick, or to tell them you changed your mind at the last moment. This is why we need to work within a reasonable time frame. I'm sorry for being so direct, but this is Antonio's best chance, maybe his last. If you say no, how long before he becomes sick too?"

Leonardo felt himself choke; hot tears stung his eyes with a sharpness equal to that of the blatant accusations of egoism, which deeply cut into his pride. He wanted to shout that it was the pollution that ate away at him, as well as the endless hours slaving at a job for a company owned by high-ranking congregation members. That it was the endless shifts spent running their machines, the same ones used to make devices that would make people like him obsolete and utterly helpless. He gave his all into such labors, only for him to leave his job at the end of his shift to have to do more work for the congregation at their events, passing out flyers or preaching or recruiting.

It wasn't just the disease that had killed his wife, but the exhaustion that was now killing him too. He was human, he and his family were people, but to the congregation they were nothing more than tools.

Leonardo would have said this and more, but all he managed was to cough for several long and painful minutes as the woman sat staring at him with her uncaring, dead eyes, waiting for him to stop before she would speak again.

"You don't have to sign." She steepled her fingers again, sitting impassively on her office chair. "You can leave and find other venues, but if you turn your back now, this is it."

Leonardo looked at the papers and the pen that waited for him to sign the deal, when he felt his cell phone vibrating. He flipped open the device, a decades old model.

Leonardo checked the caller's ID. He knew what it would be but the habit was stronger than reason, and rejected the call under the disapproving look of the adoption services clerk..

His son's future was hanging in the balance, a binary choice.

***

Leonardo had left the little office, unsure if he had made the right choice. Everything felt wrong. He felt dizzy, unbalanced as he stood in the descending lift. A couple stood by, visibly distancing themselves from him in the confines of the metal box, as if afraid of being contaminated by him.

Perhaps they were afraid of some sort of contagion; Leonardo likely looked as sick as he felt, and would likely have acted the same way if the roles were swapped. They looked young, their clothes expensive, another contrast to himself. He couldn't even begin to imagine what that felt like. Not only to be young. but to *feel* young, to have options that only wealth could provide.

Casas stumbled out when the doors opened, getting ahead of the couple, crossing the entrance and exiting the building. He couldn't tell right from left for a while, the streets outside kept twisting into a maze of light and noise until he couldn't take it anymore and he stopped, leaning against a light post and he closed his eyes. His phone vibrated in his pocket again and Leonardo answered the ring of the portable museum piece which he preserved with care.

"Hello?"

Static, and gargled voices. It could be anyone.

"Hello?"

He felt his knees giving in, his whole-body following suit, and Casas started to fall over with the phone still in his hand, his eyes too weak to read the number; they looked like braille, or morse code.

The device screamed at him as he fell into an abyss! Screeching dotted by piercing wails, a cacophony of mechanical sounds and the manic pressing of buttons that were meaningless to him.

.-. ..- -.

.-. ..- -.

.-. ..- -.

It all went away.

***

"Hey, are you okay?"

Leonardo woke up and the smell hit him like a truck. He leaned to his right and his body fought to make him vomit. He hadn't eaten yet that day, so only spit came out.

"Had a rough one too, huh? Here!"

Without questioning, Leonardo grabbed the bottle he was handed and drank deeply. He had expected water but it was beer, tepid, leaning on warm. It was far from ideal and it was likely to do him more harm than good. For now it felt better than nothing.

"I don't have much, but you can have a bit of my sandwich if it helps."

Leonardo managed to see the person in front of him then, slowly coming into focus. It was a homeless man, his hands holding half a sub to Leonardo. The bum's hands seemed clean, his face also, but the smell of sweat was strong, and two of his fingers were missing.

Leonardo refused.

"Oh, don't worry, I know a place. I'll get another one tomorrow. Take it."

His face burning with shame, his stomach growling at him, Leonardo accepted the food from the vagrant. Between it and the drink he felt some life being breathed back into him.

"Found you knocked out right there." The homeless man pointed behind him. "Name's Joe. Hope you don't mind the noise from the overpass."

It looked like they were under a bridge and Leonardo could hear the speeding cars, but they felt like something distant. Wherever he had ended up, he was not at the foot of the spotless corporate building. Likely, he had been carried away and tossed out like garbage, but he pushed the thought as far away from himself as he could manage.

Something made a noise in his pocket; he remembered holding his cell before fainting. He expected it would be the neighbors that had been taking care of Antonio for him that day.

They were sure to be asking where the hell he was, especially after he had rejected their call at the office building. He pulled out the device and flipped it open, but the screen was cracked and the text, or numbers, were indecipherable. Everything was distorted and mixed with some sort of ink from inside the phone, the plastic frame cracked and bent also.

"Haven't seen one of those in ages!" Joe laughed, sitting next to Leonardo, both their backs against a wall. "That little thing looks how I feel. I put it back in your pocket when I found you."

Leonardo put the phone to his ear; the sound was like a distant wind, muted and incomprehensible whispers. He rejected the call, turned it off and closed the lid on the cellphone. It was broken, likely beyond repair.

"I threw mine away! One good chuck and I felt lighter; I wasn't planning on going back anyhow, so it wasn't going to do me any good." Joe followed this statement by opening another beer bottle and drinking from it. He had improvised a tent on the wide sidewalk and what was likely all of his possessions were out in the open. It was mostly empty bottles and a backpack.

"Back where?" Leonardo put the phone away, thinking if he had no other way of contributing to the kindness, the least he could do was listen to Joe's story.

"You know. Life. Out there, in the factory and so on. I noticed your fingers, the burns and the scars. Mine were the same back then." Joe proudly displayed his hands, missing fingers and all. "I'm a real hand model now, even though I'm running short by a few." He waved them around. "Soft hands Joe, they call me!"

"What happened to you?"

"Oh, you know, the usual. You get sleepy or distracted and..."

"I mean, why did you leave?"

"Ah! Well, the machines taking a couple of fingers was a pretty good incentive, but there was more. You see, they had been threatening us for a while, me and some others who were getting slow. Bosses looked our way and said that they were going to replace us.

"Age caught up with us, nothing you can do about that, and when we all started getting together, asking for better conditions and stuff, so we could retire or at least do easier work because of all our years and our health, they sent people to beat us. So, I quit. Never came back and never regretted it. They don't get to make me like this and throw me away."

Leonardo held back from commenting on Joe's current living situation, and instead said:

"What about the other?"

Joe shrugged. "They're the others, I'm me. Win or lose, I was just going to get replaced anyway, thrown out from being old. Better leave than take another beating, you know?"

Leonardo didn't like it, but he understood all too well.

"I can't leave, I have a son who needs me... and I'm dying." Before Leonardo could stop himself, it all came bubbling up. "They killed my wife. Now they're killing me, and I don't know what kind of world I'm leaving behind. I don't want this for him but I don't know what to do."

Joe drank in silence, minutes were filled only by the noises from the overpass.

"Used to have a dream." Joe's eyes grew glossy, distant. "Every night for years, while I was still working at that horrible place; standing at the assembly line, and we were building something, and losing parts of us. Fingers, arms, legs.

"In the dream we just kept working and I couldn't figure out what the hell we were making. They put tubes in us, pumped our blood out to fill us with poison. Weirdest thing, just kept going and in the end, what was driving me crazy was, I had to know what we were assembling! So, in one of those dreams, I pull out the tubes and run to the end of the line, pushing past people whose faces I knew but couldn't remember when I woke up.

"I walked into a warehouse, where we piled up the stuff we were making in boxes, whatever that was we were building. I opened one of the boxes and it made some sick sense to me when I finally saw it.

"There was a person inside the box; and all the other boxes, they were all people sized, so I just knew I would find more like it. It was a woman, this one; I reached out to touch her face and it felt wrong. I pulled at it; it came off and under that was metal, all metal and blood and those missing pieces of us."

Joe went quiet, and in the back of Leonardo's mind, the woman in the box looked like the bureaucrat from the adoption agency.

"What are you trying to tell me, Joe?"

"I'm saying I've done better, but I'm not having those dreams anymore. I know what's real, and I'm getting my shit together. Probably doesn't look like it to you, but I am. Can't tell you what tomorrow looks like, but I'm going out west. It's taking me a while, having no money and all. I'm past my prime, no one has any use for me so I know my chances aren't great, but fuck it. If it's just you and your boy, right? Grab him and take off."

"I can't do that. My son..."

"Your son! Working in the line like you and me until they break him. Or getting taken away, I guess, since he doesn't have a mother any more. We're all running on a timer, and our replacements are ready to step in and keep the machine going. It's a nightmare, everything I left behind is a nightmare and this is what's real." Joe waved around them holding a now empty bottle. "But there's more to life than this. Just saying. There are places out there where a man with enough time can start over. It's too late for us to change the world, but you can change yourself. Give your boy a chance."

Joe proceeded to belch.

"Well, this was great, but I'm ready to sleep. Can't do it during the night; gets too cold. Good luck, man."

Leonardo watched as Joe retreated to his tent, zipping the flaps behind him.

***

It was late. Leonardo got his son to bed, turned off the lights and went to his own room only to find he could not sleep. He sat on the corner of his bed and looked outside the window.

It faced other buildings, their windows dark but for a single couple with the lights on, drapes open. A lone man sat watching TV on the third floor. His living room was blue from the light of the screen. Leonardo couldn't tell the man's expression, if he was sad, happy or neutral; to him the man was a blur in a tank top, a faceless lump of flesh on a couch. He was someone dying in the quiet of their living room, with only a machine for company.

In another, a woman was smoking, looking outside her window. Her face was clearer to him, closer and better illuminated. She looked tired, as tired as he was.

Leonardo closed his eyes and thought back to the papers. Again, the pen was in his hand and the decision was waiting for him to choose: to sign or not to sign.

He flipped the cellphone open and turned it on, placed it to his heart, not sure what to expect. Silence is all there was to be found. No ghosts or beeps, not his wife's voice or an angry call to make demands

Looking again at it, Leonardo realized the phone was dead. Not just out of battery, but too broken to function at all. He broke down too and cried, holding back his sobs so his son wouldn't hear him. His wife had bought him the phone.

When the next day came, what would he say to his child? How would he say it?

In a fetal position on top of his bed, too tired to crawl under the sheets and holding the broken device, he tried to imagine a small house in the countryside. Leonardo closed his eyes hard, and focused on the sun, the trees, the smell of the fields. It was like in his youth, when his grandparents had been alive.

They were hard people, from a harder life. A life that raced them by, making them second class citizens when they couldn't work like they used to, or understand the technologies that seemed to dominate the world.

Theirs had not been an idyllic life, but they had raised their children and even helped raise the grandchildren. Now their world and their people were all lost to time. Mourned little, if at all, and only half remembered; those who aided in their destruction, covering the trail of their misdeeds with meaningless sympathetic words. Crying masks covering hardened and apathetic faces.

Without knowing if he was still awake or asleep, Leonardo dreamt. He dreamt of burying his old cell phone like a dead pet, and then gently holding his son by the hand and walking away from the glass towers of the city center. Leonardo dreamt it all becoming distant, the noises and smells that made him sick, the people who looked at their neighbors without seeing them. Together, father and son walked towards a glorious sunrise, green fields opening ahead of them both.

SWEET CHILD

Everyone knew about the killings. The papers made sure of it, because of how brutal they were. The people who had stumbled on the carcasses put the blame on some punk kids going too far, or wild animal attacks to explain all those deaths. There had been dozens of them.

They started with the cattle from the farm's miles out, but the killings had gotten closer. The killer was getting bolder the nearer to the city they got. They started killing strays, then pets started to go missing. This is when I lost my dog. My mother told me it had run away, but I didn't believe her. Not when more pets had been gone from backyards and even from inside their owner's homes. Some were never to be found again, others found in pieces some weeks later.

Wishful thinking was never enough, and prayers always went unheard. It was time for action, so me and my friends prepared ourselves for the hunt. There was Jack, who had always been the tallest of us, Georgie whose dad had shot himself that past summer, and finally Rivers, whose first name I never learned. Then there was me.

We were all about fifteen years old back then, but had grown rough. We had to stand for ourselves almost as soon as we had learned to stand at all. We thought this must be another monster, another sadist asshole building up courage to imitate the guy that had been caught the year before. This was another serial killer. Everyone had refused to believe the last guy was real until he had been caught; it had been too late by then. We weren't about to wait around for it to escalate, not when the killings had gotten too close to our homes. We rode our bicycles around, armed with baseball bats and knives.

We even had a gun. At the time that didn't horrify me at all; though it would years later when I had to start to dig up these memories. You see, my previous therapist, like yourself, kept pushing me to spill the beans on childhood stuff. Just digging, and digging. *How do you feel about it? Why do you think that is?* She squeezed until she got this little pearl I'm about to share, and after that she sent me to you.

Anyway, I think that the fact there were worse things than guns being sold on the streets, the way things were back then, made us all numb to violence up to a point. That was probably why we just took all of it in stride. We weren't going to let some sick fuck kill our dogs, or our families, or us. We picked up our weapons and started doing the rounds, nearly getting ourselves caught a couple of times. When it's for self-defense, you don't think it's really fucked that a bunch of kids are walking around armed.

One day we finally see something, but not what we had expected. It was on four legs, chasing something. We had expected some mutt, but this looked like some animal that had been let loose by the owner. Maybe the rumor about an escaped exotic animal was true after all. We chased it into the alley and saw, scared stiff, as it tore something apart in moments. I remember the smell, all of us holding our breath, just staring at it.

I realized it wasn't eating its kill. It was playing with the dead body, spilling the insides that it had torn out of some poor stray cat. This was out back of a bar called Rocking Horse, a bar I had gone to many times, so I could help my dad find his way back home after a bad night.

We couldn't see the thing clearly because it was getting dark, and the shadows had grown darker, the horrible smells from that back alley making us cry ourselves blind, but I swear to God it looked like a monkey I had seen on the TV once. I had to look it up later because I couldn't remember what they were called.

It looked like a *mandrill*. When I first got a half decent look at it, that's what I thought. But I was wrong; I just don't have anything else I can think of, even now, that comes any closer. It looked so wrong that I still feel my stomach drop when I think about it. If there had been a sane explanation for it, what it had been when we first saw it, it would have to be that. A wild animal that didn't belong in our little town, that looked alien and smelled like death. Whatever that thing was, it was a killer and we knew it right then. Someone had to stop it.

Jack, the biggest guy in our little gang, stepped into the alley as quietly as he could. I held myself back not to call him back. It wouldn't do, to have the alley killer notice us. Better it kept playing half hidden by shadows of the two dumpsters.

We heard the noises that the thing made, human-like, all mumbled up and a little high pitched, which made it sound like a kid. You know, like about when they start to learn how to talk. The thing was all hunched and looked smaller than we had expected. It was covered in dark red hair and it was *filthy*. It was also so focused on playing around with the mess it made that it didn't even seem to hear us.

It made noises, all the talking with grunts and hisses, while using the bits it tore off the cat, playing with them like they were dolls. Jack came close enough to grab the thing when it stopped moving. It didn't turn to face him.

Georgie was the one who brought the gun, the same one his dad had used to blow his own head with a year before, but don't ask me why or how he kept something like that. Georgie had his finger itching to pull the trigger, and was doing his best to hold still. He tried to aim, waiting for the right moment to shoot whatever the thing was. River was trying to calm us down before we scared it or Georgie ended up shooting Jack by mistake. We just held still when the thing got quiet.

After a while, we saw the little monster carefully laying the limbs on the ground and picking up the rest of the cat's corpse to hold it close to its chest. It started rocking back and forth while petting the lolling head of the stray, mumbling to it in a broken singing voice, sounding like someone trying to recite a nursery rhyme with a mouth full of eggs. Having seen and waited enough, Jack actually stepped back to get out of the way.

Georgie couldn't hold it any longer, he was shaking and he smelled of sweat so bad I almost forgot the smell of the garbage. He aimed as best he could and pulled the trigger on the thing. He told me later that he had been practicing. The ape almost flew forward with the force of the blast, and I swear to this day I could feel the blast shake me too.

It was like a fireball, the smoke and light blinded us, and the noise was deafening. I felt for a moment it was over and that whatever it had been, that freak couldn't hurt anyone again.

It really was just a moment, because the damn monster bounced back furious, and we knew we had fucked up. It stood, and in a blink, it had turned on us. The little monster grabbed the back of its head, a head that should have been blown to pieces, with both hands. And it was screaming. Georgie shot the second time, and I'm sure he missed by a thousand miles. The thing ran at us screaming, bleeding and furious.

"MA!" it said "MAAAAA!" and bounced off the nearest wall ready to tear Jack's face when Georgie must have gotten lucky and hit it with his third shot.

It flew back again, with a hit to the chest that sprayed blood and fur on Jack and Georgie, while I fell on my ass completely terrified. River kept shouting "Fuck! Fuck! Fuck!"

The thing which I started to doubt being an ape, hit the wall with its back and fell into the one of the open garbage dumpsters. There was blood everywhere, pieces of guts and brains flying around like confetti.

Rivers took the gun from Georgie's hands before he shot himself (or one of us). Jack picked up my baseball bat and ran to the dumpster ready to swing at the thing inside. It started to throw garbage at us, quickly climbing out of the dumpster and racing at him on all fours.

Jack swung the bat with all his strength and hit it on the side I heard the sound of something breaking as one of its arms turned in a way it wasn't meant to; but the fucker buried its dirty fingers on Jack's shoulder, and bit him in the face. I panicked and Georgie threw up. Rivers was the one who ended up saving Jack by pulling out a spray can and a lighter and setting fire to the hairy thing. It let go of Jack, who fell on his back holding his face. Then, the thing ran off on all fours, screaming and leaving a trail of burned fur, blood, and trash for us to follow.

Back then, the town was much smaller. Outside of it were just miles of farms, so people were spread out few and far between. I don't blame any of our parents for letting us go out and about the way we did; they were all busy working themselves to the bone to keep us fed.

We made enough noise to wake up the dead, but the nearest bunch was a group of factory workers, still in uniform and dirty with grease. They were already drunk, making their way to the bar to continue drinking away their problems when they saw us. It felt like that had to be the end of it, with Jack bleeding and the rest of us shitting ourselves scared. But Jack looked at me, half his face covered in blood, his left cheek missing, and screamed at us to go and kill it.

Rivers started running. The men knew for sure something was wrong and started running at us, so I helped Georgie up and ran after Rivers. Jack screamed at the men to help him and got their attention long enough they didn't manage to stop us. We followed the blood, which grew thinner, but the smell of burnt fur got stronger. I don't know how long we ran but it got darker and must have been late when Rivers finally stopped in front of a rusty gate that opened to a path.

It led to an abandoned house and I couldn't see shit past the overgrown grass of the front yard. After a while, we could hear the weak noises the thing made, and found no one had followed us. The nearest houses were far and spread out enough that people in them probably couldn't see us that night if they looked out of their windows.

We marched up the path and found the thing laying down by the front door of the house, which was chained shut but had a wide and round window at the top that opened to the darkness inside the house. By the blood, the thing had tried climbing up and in with just one arm, but fell back down landing on the steps leading to the door.

It stayed there breathing hard, sitting with its back against the door, one small hand still holding to one of the chains, its arm too long for the body it belonged to, still mostly covered in fur. It looked up to us with a hate I had never seen before in my life and never saw again. Its face was pale and bloodless, with two small shiny wet eyes. It had a face like a child, but seeing it, even in the dark, and even with all the burn marks, it wasn't human. And it didn't look like any fucking monkey I had ever seen in a zoo. It was like someone had glued a bunch of parts together, and then painted over to try to disguise it as just one thing. It didn't even feel like something from this world. It spit at us and hissed, then grimaced with a mouth full of sharp mismatched teeth.

"End of the road, you hairy bastard," Rivers said, and the crazy fuck pulled out Georgie's' gun and aimed it at the thing.

It panicked, and I realized later that whatever it was it was smart enough to know what the gun meant now, and it knew to be afraid of it. "Ma! Ma!" it started to shout back at us, all the while pushing itself harder against the door and rattling the chains. What happened next we never saw coming.

Rivers would hit it for sure, but my dizziness wasn't the rush from knowing it was going to be over. What got me holding my breath, was something moving inside the house.

I jumped just in time to grab Rivers, who had gotten too close and we both stepped back. A huge hand shot out of the round window hole in the door and nearly got us. Georgie screamed and ran off. Rivers and I, we just stayed there staring at it, at how massive, calloused and fur covered that hand was. It grabbed the smaller monster and pulled it up and inside the house, into the shadows. We stared at that window like it was a black hole ready to suck us in also. We couldn't see anything inside, nothing clear at least, but we could hear it well enough as it began to sob.

"Oohhh, what have they done to you? Those animals."

Just like that, in perfect English, but I couldn't believe it. I didn't want to believe those things could actually talk. Talk like people, even if the voice sounded wrong, like God had made a mistake bigger than the human race.

"I don't know what you two are, but your little monster is tearing apart anything he can grab. If you can understand what I'm telling you, you better give me one good reason not to burn the house down with you in it."

I just stared at Rivers, and I could hear that from inside the dilapidated house came further sobbing but no pleading and no explanations.

"My poor boy. My sweet boy. Ohh, my sweet boy. So good. So good."

There was a muffled cry, followed by disgustingly loud wet noises and bones being crushed. We had enough then. We both took off from that damned porch.

Rivers took a few more steps back. He still had that spray can with him, and the crazy fuck started setting it on fire, heating it up at the bottom with the lighter. He then tossed it, timed the shot and blasted at the can as it flew into the darkness. The explosion must have been heard everywhere in town, and the horrible screams from inside the house as well. A ball of fire spread flames everywhere. We turned and ran away followed by the sound of the *mother* slamming its body against the door. We heard the rattling of the chains followed by the sound of the house crumbling on itself, hopefully crushing and burning away everything inside it.

I lost contact with the guys after that night. First a few weeks went by, then years. No one ever asked us anything, or suspected us. Something still messes with me though.

The news talked about the fire. How the firefighters found old stuff, animal and human bones, things dead long before the fire. But not the mother and the cub we killed.

Can't stop thinking about it. Where did the bodies go?

TOADIE

A previous version of TOADIE was read on the Lunatics Library Episode 32: Goblin Horror Stories

1966, Portugal.

It happened on a Friday, during the holidays. In a little house out north, close by the river, Julia couldn't keep the baby quiet, no matter what she did. "Please, please!" She begged. André watched, also exhausted, though likely not as much; he wasn't the mother, after all. Without rising from the sofa, he raised both hands, posing as if in an oil painting. Some biblical figure waiting to receive baby Jesus in his arms.

"I'll hold him."

"No." Julia's reply was short, dry, and gave no room for debate. "What kind of mother would I be? What will our neighbors say when we get back? When I can't keep him quiet?"

André curled on the sofa, and fell asleep despite the crying. What woke him was the thunder. As he jerked to a sitting position, his sight blurry from sleep, the door slammed closed.

"God. Julia, what happened?"

"I didn't want to wake you." She adjusted her hair. All of her was dripping wet from head to toe, and she held a bundle close to her chest.. "A walk. I went for a walk. With the baby. It worked."

André was filled with a moment of panic, staring at the wet bundle. He peeked, carefully, pushing aside some of the fabric. The child looked up from within.

The babe, Rafael, was still, but his eyes were open and full of life. He smiled at his father, who sighed with relief.

"I don't know what possessed you." He said as quietly as he could, not to scare the babe. "But I'm begging you not to run out in the rain with our son."

"It wasn't running then!" Julia replied in a hoarse whisper of her own. She took Rafael upstairs, bathed him and dried him. Afterwards, she returned the boy to his father so she could do the same for herself.

"Do you want to sleep now?" He soothed the child as best he could, though Rafael seemed to be in a pleasant state of half sleep already. The baby cooed, and reached with one small hand. André smiled back and allowed the baby to hold to his index finger. "That's such a strong grip you have! That's my boy."

He walked around the living room of the comfy country house. All manner of memorabilia hung from the walls, from paintings, to black and white photos from locals. Dead people; ghosts for the better half of a decade. Some blew horns that also hung from the walls, made of the semi-curved horns of bulls. They were joined by metal bells that once rang from the necks of sheep, and the clattering of horseshoes.

Picking up one such horseshoe, André tried to show it to the baby. "Look," he started, but would not finish. As soon as he brought it close to the face of the child, the babe began to scream. The face contorted horribly, skin folding upon folding, the head of a tiny old man.

"What happened?" Julia started to run downstairs wearing only her robe, and André threw away the horse shoe to some corner of the floor. By the time Julia was next to them, her hair still wet, their son had calmed down. "There, there. Mommy's here. Don't cry, darling."

Julia held her son in her arms and rocked her boy gently, humming a lullaby. She looked at her husband accusingly, but said nothing. Once the boy was asleep, they went to bed. The rain continued, but waned from a downpour down to a light shower. Night sounds made their way into the bedroom, the wind, the nearby river, and the cracking and chirping of toads.

André fell asleep to dreams of men and women with frog heads, dancing and singing in their amphibian language, plucking objects the dreamer could not see from wicker baskets, and devouring them whole.

***

Two weeks went by. They were back in their own little house, close to a different river, in the old town full of homes that had been built and rebuilt since medieval days. It was still within the capital, which made it a city life, though their neighborhood reminded them of the country in many ways.

"Peek-a-boo!" The little boy laughed with delight, a contagious warmth in the sound. "I'm here!" Julia hid her face again. "Where did I go?" The laughing stopped.

"Peek-a-boo!" The smile was held for a moment of surprise and disbelief and her body contorted; her face became stuck in the rigid agony of a scream.

"What happened!?" André rushed to the sunny kitchen, the spring warmth and the smell of flowers carried by the breeze both mixed with the smell of cooking. He had been quietly working on some numbers in a notebook. It had been his turn to figure out how to stretch the couple's salary that month, that routine of the adult mathematics of survival, in which they both had become professional athletes.

"The baby! The baby is gone! Oh, God!" She looked around in a panic, touched the empty chair grasping at air "The baby is gone!!"

"The window!" André jumped out of the kitchen window and started running, the mother staring out and completely lost. She saw it then, moving past the neighbor's doors, a small figure wearing a red coat and hood, the top of which formed the point of a conical shape. This stranger practically flew over flights of steps while holding the baby, and running down the ancient cobbled street. André could only follow, close in pursuit.

Julia lost them as they turned the corner of a house, then ran to pick up the phone and call the police. Julia sobbed, her tears streaking down her face and ruining her makeup. It wasn't her fault, she said to herself. Yet she couldn't help but feel immense guilt.

***

The figure was small, a child if he had to guess, and André could only guess. He could only assume it was not one of the neighbors' kids because it was dressed in dirty red rags, too filthy for someone in a nice neighborhood to allow their children to wear. *It just wasn't proper,* he reasoned. He shouted as he raced after the boy.

All his neighbors came out of their doors and windows, to stare at the madman racing past homes, shops and cafés, and eventually out and away, past the road full of cars and towards the river, and the docks.

Every time he was close enough to the ragamuffin to grab it, it dodged him. Why would no one help him? It felt like a nightmare that he couldn't wake up from, trapped in the chase that would never end.

The sun was setting by the time the ragamuffin started to slow down. It tripped and for a disorienting, panicked moment, the father feared for his boy. The kidnapper rolled to land on their back, preventing the worst from happening by holding the baby Rafael close to their chest. André felt like vomiting up at that moment, so scared and out of breath, with his legs shaking and almost numb. He managed not to, but only then did he realize how far they had run.

Once at the docks, the chase continued until they were close to massive containers filled with all manners of stock. The figure trod behind those metal monoliths. It seemed the dock was empty but for them, and the little red boy stopped at last, finding himself cornered. Trembling in terror, André approached the small figure. Rafael seemed to be fine, and was happily cooing while still being held by whoever had taken him.

"Stop," he muttered at the kidnapper, "please. My son. Give me my son."

He barely had any breath in his lungs; saying the words seemed to take more than he had to give. The kidnapper slowly sat up and pulled back his red hood. What André saw stopped him in place because it was so strange.

It may have been a child who had taken his son, but nothing was normal about the child that looked up at him. The boy had big amphibian eyes too big for its head and wet with tears.. The skin was pale, sickly, covered not so much with hair but dark fur. Pointy ears framed a swollen head that made it look cartoonish. The boy-creature blinked up at André, big shiny tears rolling down the horrid face and it croaked hoarsely at him.

"Please," it said, "I'm sorry, please let me go. It's my brother."

André got closer to the child, but he felt sicker the closer he drew. All the running had driven him to the point of fainting, and now he was staring, unable to understand what the toad child meant.

"That's... That's my son."

The creature shook its head, blinking hard to clear its massive eyes while it held the baby closer. "She took him!" It said with a child's voice, whining and speaking with difficulty as if it was still learning how. "She took him! I asked her to come back, she didn't stop! She tricked me!" The father was utterly lost, too confused to make heads or tails of what was going on. "Don't tell her, please don't tell her. Say you lost me. You can't trust her, you can't!"

"What are you saying?"

"She lied to you! She took my brother and told you lies! Look at him, look!"

The father looked and through the daze he realized the babe was wrong. It had never really resembled him, but it was now clear the thing was froglike, as the older child was. He had been tricked.

"But why?"

"I don't know! I don't know. Please let me go. Please?"

He was a broken man, incapable of doing anything but falling to his knees. He hid his face in his hands, and rocked back and forth, powerless. The frog child hesitated only a moment before creeping around the desolate father, then ran off towards the river.

What had happened that Friday night, out north during the downpour? Why had Julia come back with a child not her own, a child made to appear like theirs?

André couldn't understand how neither of them had known. This was real, it had happened, and at least one of them must have suspected. One of the parents must have known. The child had been so quiet.

Until André had shown the horseshoe to the changeling.

***

They found him covered in scratches and standing dumbly, his hands still covering his face. Local law collected him and wrote off the incident as temporary madness.

"Let me see him!" Julia was desperate. Much as she feared it, she had to know. A chill ran up her spine and nestled on the back of her head. Once there, it whispered into her ears that this was punishment for an unspoken sin. Julia forced his hand away from his face and was met by vacant eyes. She held her husband in her arms and cried.

***

Back north, past a comely country house, past the river, under bushes and lost somewhere in the mountains where it was nearly always cold, red-hooded creatures danced and cavorted as they croaked their songs to one another. They had rescued one of their youngest and found him a brother to pair him with: a human baby boy, who laughed and applauded. His parents were forgotten, and he in turn had been dressed in a red coat and a red cap, the dress of his foster people. He sat next to the changeling who looked like him, sometimes, and who he would always call brother.

You're the Sheriff

It's not easy to deal with authority, especially when it lives in your home with you.

Tommy's dad was the sheriff, which had sounded fun when he had liked cowboys. At age twelve, getting close to almost thirteen, the illusion broke. The fact was that the sheriff didn't need or want him as a deputy. His dad, never again his hero, always had his gun on his holster and his badge on his chest. His dad was not the hero but the villain; that lesson was taught often.

All the other kids knew, but could do nothing. After all, they weren't adults. Their parents knew, but they weren't the sheriff, and the other lawmen knew better than to stick their noses in each other's businesses. It was another lesson Tommy learned young, that people with badges are their own kind of people with their own special laws.

Laws they have to follow to avoid making each other mad.

"If I had a gun, I would shoot him," Tommy told his best friend, whose name was Eddie. "He would never hit me again."

Eddie couldn't voice his support, since he was mute. Instead he nodded and pretended to take aim, then shoot at something in the distance with a finger gun.

"Yeah... You wouldn't tell on me, would you?" Eddie wouldn't tell a soul, of course. Not from being mute, but due to a kind-hearted nature that Tommy starved for. A kindness Tommy had been deprived of for as long as he could walk and talk. Eddie was worried for his friend, and didn't want to see him hurt.

One day, should that day come, Tommy would need to get every detail right. He would have only one chance. If his father caught him, a deadly beating would ensue. Worse than the beating he had given Tommy's mom the one time she had tried to fight back. Tommy could barely remember her now, how she had always smelled of apples. How she had loved him.

Their home had been empty of such things for as long Tommy could remember clearly. Fruits had been replaced with tasteless, microwavable meals. Love had been replaced with nothing. Life was empty of color and meaning beyond tense violence. Color had been carved out of their home, filled in turn with the grayish fumes of cars parked outside. The only familiar sounds were of a TV that was only allowed to be used for sports games and strange news shows, hosted by angry middle aged men. They seemed to be in constant anger, at the zenith of which they resembled the sheriff. Tommy would only sneak watch a random cartoon when his dad wasn't home.

He had grown to hate that TV, and the walls of the house itself, which felt like those of a prison. Tommy learned to spend much of his time outside.

When thinking back to his mother, the boy never stopped to wonder how his old man had gotten away with it. How he could have escaped punishment from beating another adult until they had broken. Until they had either died or left - Tommy was never sure which it had been. Maybe the lesson about people with badges making their own rules had a truth to it which really did reach beyond the confines of their sad, lonely trailer park.

Tommy hadn't made his mind yet as to when he was going to do it, or how. Some deeper understanding, a voice that told him to prioritize survival would keep him from rushing it. The voice manifested nearly every time he heard his dad snore loud enough that the neighbors probably could hear him.

Tommy knew he would have to wait. Some night perhaps, a night in which his dad was so drunk that waking him up by accident would be impossible. Maybe Tommy could set it up so anyone who heard a shot might think a robber did it. It could even be an accident, at the end of a day of drunken shouting and stumbling about, for which the sheriff had a reputation. Accidents happen. The way the sheriff told it, Tommy's grandfather had been killed in an accident. They had been out in the woods and another hunter shot the old man. The killer was never found.

"Would you take me hunting, dad?"

Tommy never asked for anything, and the question made the sheriff raise an eyebrow. *He knows*, Tommy panicked. *He knows!*

"Too busy for that."

Tommy's dad had turned his attention back to the TV. Tommy could imagine there might have been a hint of shame or maybe even regret in the man's voice. Had it really been an accident? The sheriff had been a young man then, but old enough that he had been on that hunting trip, holding a weapon of his own.

"You would be no good anyway."

With that dismissive insult from his father, the boy felt an immense relief,; though he knew better than to show it.

***

Spring came, and on a day as hot as any on a Summer, Tommy and Eddie decided to make a after school detour. The sheriff had been called for some business and was bound to be late, so Tommy had time all to himself.

The boys decided to buy candy using some of Eddie's allowance. Tommy didn't get any money from his dad and he would not risk stealing some.

The little convenience store was welcoming enough, despite having nothing special about it. As ancient and decrepit as it was, a relic from an age thirty years past obsolete, it stood with the certainty of a temple. It was ready to take the money of any passerby as if it was the tithe of a pilgrim on the road to Jerusalem, and the old woman who worked the counter was this temple's sole priestess.

Sometimes both boys scored free goodies that were past the expiration date. The lady who owned the place had to throw it out anyway.

"Just a little something for my favorite customers."

They were her least favorite actually, but Sabina, now in the latter half of her sixties, found that seeing these two familiar faces was better than none. She sat most of her days behind the counter in a state of a decades-long abandonment. As time passed, she dealt more with strangers who dropped off the road for directions, snacks and a bathroom break than with any of the locals. She lived in exile.

Though she would never admit it to herself, there was probably a deeper reason she tossed candies to the children. A bruise, or black eye, or the sense of abandonment emanating from both children. Though the latter might have been her projecting her own feelings. Some deep core part of Sabina, not yet fully hardened by age and remorse, found the memories of her own bruises not so distant.

Her husband had not worn a badge, and he never threatened her with the gun he had kept close to him for as long as he had lived. Still, for most of her years he had beaten her and the scales had always tipped more to his side than to hers. She had not cried for him at the funeral, and the few who attended judged her cold. Sabina had been as uncaring as the snow that had covered the grave dirt, barren as their marriage had been. She would have burned his ashes and dumped him somewhere, but a proper burial had been the Christian thing to do.

Sabina also thought it would be less suspicious that way. She had finally been free of him; putting up with one more humiliation had been better than drawing attention to his death. If people realized she had made the fetid old drunk overdose on sleeping pills, they might feel sympathy, but would also condemn her.

On that spring day, hot enough to be mistaken for summer, the boys walked in to find no one behind the counter. There were no other customers, and the shelves were ransacked. Looking around, the boys knew something was wrong. Eddie gestured that they should leave when sirens blasted like trumpets announcing judgment day, so loud they hurt.

Knowing the pigs were closing in, Tommy could feel a fresh beating coming up in his way, for simply being in the wrong place at the wrong time. They both ran behind a display made of cans piled up into a pyramid. Behind it they could both crouch and disappear completely. They heard the door opening and the careful steps of whoever walked in.

"Sabina! It's me!"

Of all the people who could have gotten there first, of course it would have been Tommy's dad. Anyone else would have followed etiquette and called for Mrs. Terrance rather than defaulting to a first name basis, but he was the sheriff after all. Why bother with such details?

"Sab? We got the call…"

Tommy covered his mouth with both hands, and Eddie did the same, scared that their breathing would be too loud. They heard the sheriff move to the counter and they both moved further back. Tommy's dad came into view and they just barely avoided being seen by him, as he went around the counter slowly and carefully, trying to get to the back of the store.

"Say something, you old cu–"

There was a bang, the sound of glass shattering, and the thud of a body hitting the ground.

A distressed and very thin man, shaking and greasy looking, walked out to the sheriff's body. He pointed down where Tommy's dad had fallen, and shot twice more. The thin man leaned on the counter, still holding the pistol in one hand while combing his long oily hair with the other.

"Fuck," was all he said.

He moved over and bent down, going out of sight. The boys heard him searching for something, gibbering swear words and stringing together excuses. Then, the stranger just stopped and almost ran out from behind the counter, not paying attention to anything else.

They heard him walk further and further away, and in a few moments the man was gone, never to be found again. He was lost to the world like Tommy's mother was lost to him, a half-formed memory and a smell and little more.

Eddie was the first to peek, leaning from the door to see if the man was truly gone once they could no longer hear him. Satisfied they were alone, he gestured to Tommy that it was safe. They left their hideout and went behind the counter. They found the sheriff bleeding from two bullet wounds: one in his shoulder and the other on his chest, where his heart would have been if he'd had one.

The robber had taken the sheriff's gun, and Eddie, looking pale, held Tommy by the shoulder. He pointed to a door they couldn't see before, that led to a store room. There was blood on the floor, the fluorescent light reflected by blood soaked disarranged packages

"I'm not going there, Ed. He probably shot the old lady the same way he shot my dad."

Tommy crouched and resisted the temptation to spit in his old man's face. He unpinned the blood-sprayed badge with some difficulty, and held it up to the light from the shattered window. He wished he had been the one shooting his old man, but this would have to do. The engraved star was a treasure to keep him warm through the years to come.

A wheeze startled Tommy, who looked back down and shouted. He jumped back, scared, dropping the badge. His dad was still alive. His breathing was shallow, his eyes open.

"The car," he said with a mouth full of blood that oozed from his lips. "Call... help."

Tommy remembered a rare, almost tender moment. His father, only once, as far as he could remember, had driven him around in the patrol car. He had shown Tommy what it was like to cruise about, who he interacted with, and how the radio worked. He had been a different man that day, still a brute, but seemingly a happy one.

Then, the boy remembered the beatings and the drinking. Tommy's face contorted in anger, changing into something so scary that Eddie had to look away.

"I'm dying..." and before he could say another word Tommy put his hands on his father's mouth and nose, doing his best to stop him from breathing.

He pushed both hands down, blood and snot running under his palms as the dying sheriff's eyes opened wide, bulging out. His old man's face changed colors as he bled and suffocated, a dying chameleon. Even as he died, he was furious,. but unable to raise his hand against the boy and remind him of his place in nature. Tommy looked his dad in the eye and held his hands firmly in place. He was the sheriff now, and he didn't need guns or badges. He didn't even need the large, hairy hands of an adult.

Tommy was the law for the first time in his life, and had he been able to, he would have made his father say it, to acknowledge the succession.

"You're the sheriff, Tommy." He had imagined his father saying to him, fearing for his own worthless life, a gun aimed at his wide chest. "You're the sheriff. Don't rush it, son. Let's talk." Tommy had always known it would never happen, not like how he dreamt; but the fantasy had breathed hope into him during his darkest hours.

After many long minutes, the man stopped struggling, and a terrible smell followed as his life and the contents of his bowls escaped his body.

Slow, shaking, and smeared in the blood of his father, Tommy moved his hands to his dad's chest and shoulder, then pressed his palms down, right where the bullet holes were. He smeared his father's face before he stood again, made sure his hands touched the eyelids which he closed. Tommy touched the cheeks, the forehead and the hair. He held his father's neck and held the dead man's face to his chest. A silent and cold mimicry, the pretense of grief.

He looked back at Eddie, who was sitting on the floor, his hands covering his ears and his eyes full of tears, his face turned away.

"You said you wouldn't tell," Tommy reminded his friend out loud, "but if anyone asks, I tried stopping the bleeding. Okay? I tried."

Eddie nodded slowly, understanding perfectly what might happen if he ever did anything else.

"Let's go. We have to radio for help."

Tommy picked up the badge again and stood up, waving for Eddie to follow him out of the store.

ABOUT THE AUTHOR

J.R. Santos is a Portuguese author who decided to return to writing in 2019, and has since then made every effort to be published.

Seeking the surreal, the author has found few compatible opportunities for most of his work, counting only a handful of short story publications up to this point. If you have recommendations, or want to ask the author about writing a story for a project of yours, be it a zine or a book, reach out to customercareskeleton@gmail.com.

Some other publications featuring the author include the anthologies: *Archive of the Odd, Issue 1, Annus Horribilis, Well, This is Tense* and *That Old House: The Bathroom*.

You can buy *Time is a Temple,* the author's previous collection of short stories on any online retailer, or look up a digital copy in your local library.

If you enjoyed this collection, please leave a review for this book at your usual review site of choice, recommend it to a friend, etc.

ACKNOWLEDGEMENTS

I want to thank all those who shared their time and kindness with me. Those who read earlier versions of the stories, and to both Cat and Eduardo who have done absolutely wonderful work.

Thanks to you, this book is an object of both love and pride.

Printed by Amazon Italia Logistica S.r.l.
Torrazza Piemonte (TO), Italy

52882466R00059